ChoirBoy

A Novel

By

Barry Alston Ray

ChoirBoy
By Barry Alston Ray

Published By: SixN1 Publishing

ISBN: 978-1-09833-856-5

TO CONTACT THE AUTHOR
Please send all emails to:
sixn1publishing@gmail.com
talent@sixn1ent.com
www.choirboythenovel.com
www.sixn1ent.com

This Book is Dedicated To:

Carrie Mae Leagiton

Sylvester Alston1

Viola Allen

Dayvon M. Alston

Alice Stinson

James Eaddy Jr.

Cora Mae Walker

Special Thanks

Praise God from whom all blessings flow! God, you are awesome! Thank you so very much for your great love for me. For being everything you stated in your word that you'd be. Thank you Jesus for Calvary! Thank you for what you entrusted in me for the masses. I won't let you down!

To the best mother, period, Carrie E. Alston: Thank you doesn't seem enough. You are truly amazing in every sense of the word! Thank you for believing in me when I lost it all and recovery seemed nowhere in sight. It's your prayers that I stand here today! I love you!

To my brothers Lee & Robert: I truly appreciate the both of you. We may go at it but I wouldn't trade either of you for nothing (well, maybe a few Grammys) lol. Just kidding. Love you both.

My sister in-law Connie: Thank you, thank you, thank you! You are a Godsend. Thank you for coming in and assisting in this life changing transformation! Love ya!

To the family as a whole; y'all are the greatest. I appreciate each of you for your own unique gifts and abilities: Desaun, Dequan, Gerard, Antione, Tiesha, Charles & Maggie Hale, Charles Hale Jr., Lamar, Deandre, W. Lorenzo Alston and anyone I forgot within the family please charge it to my head and not my heart.

Alicia Corbin, El Wilkerson, Mildred Wilkerson and Donatien Lake Jr I could write a page for each of you easily. I thank God for the love and bond we share. Each and every one of you not only enhance my personal life but also the life of SixN1. I appreciate everything you do that helps bring this vision to a reality. This Time!!! Let's get it!!!!

David Quinones, man when I say us linking was divinely orchestrated, it's an understatement. Bro, thank you for seeing in me what others couldn't or rather wouldn't. For pushing me beyond the break. We got this and the world is about to know it. Love you, Bro.

Gerard Victor you are another divine set-up. I cannot thank you enough first for the initial opportunity on Jadakiss' "Kisses To The Sky" video. My career went to the next level literally! Then for everything else that transpired after. Thank you for being a man of your word. It's been a pleasure working with you and I'm so ready for the world to see the work!

The Don from Yonkers, N.Y. Jada kiss for the opportunity to play the diamond buyer in Kisses To The Sky music video who spoke prophetic words over my career saying "You are going to be as big as Denzel Washington". I appreciate you.

Curtis "50" Jackson for the opportunity to contribute my acting ability in two of his Tv shows "Power" and "For Life. Thanks for your encouragement and reminding me that my returning to Sing Sing Correctional Facility to film as a free man is a testament of my success and great things to come.

Adham McGuire aka Ant Morgan. Man, it's crazy! From day one on set we bonded and the rest is history. Your support and love for me never has to be questioned.

Thank you for gracing the cover of my debut literary offering. The best is yet to come!

My Paster Superintendent Gerald Wayne Smith. Thank you so very much for the example you continuously display. Thank you for the push and support that there is nothing I cannot do. I appreciate you and Lady Elect Cynthia D Smith! Thank you, thank you, thank you!!

Paula James-Johnson, one of my oldest and dearest friends. Nope, I'm lying; my sister! (God knows what you need). Thank you for the decades of love and loyalty. Love you beyond words!

Margaret P. Bean. You know I cannot stand you, right? Naw, I thank God for you! Thank you for taking a chance on me in The Gamechanger Stage Play. It's been on since. Love you and the world is about to know your name!

Lyd & Miesha Edmond. OMG! Thank God for the both of you. I appreciate you more than I can fully express!

Donnell & Sahraya Williams! Thank you, I love you both and I'm ready to show the world what we got!

Dashawn Washington you are truly the lil' brother I always wanted. Even with all the cutting up we do your support is crystal clear. Thank you for always holding me down. Love you dude.

Rasheem Pittman thank you for ALWAYS keeping me laced! I'm taking you to the masses! Just keep what you make me exclusive! Lol.
Samara Miller, my sister we have come a long way! I thank you for always holding a brother down from day one

like a big sister should. Love you and those red bottoms are coming!!!

Ok, this is getting as long as the book, so the following I love each of you and I'm grateful for the special love and support you give me: Earl & Monique Whitfield, Kyare & Starline Starks, Pastor Gilbert Pickett, Pastor David Wright, Stephanie Holloway, Ramon & Chloe Adams, Stephanie Alexandra Charles, Dina Joyner, Andrea Dialect, KiKi Washington, Bridgette Wesley, Bridgette Lunce Grimes, Cecelia Eaddy (every Eaddy), Jamar White, Terrance McCanty, Amir Robinson, Kyla McClendon, Pastor Quantrell Smith, Yolanda Braithwaite, Yolanda McCloud, Barbara Jackson, Lavette Meredith, Mattrel Smith, Vincent Scott, Andre Apparicio, Rev. Corrine Summers, Rev. Linda VanAlstyne, Rev. Iris Wadell, the entire Sister Code Stage Play, Joseph Brooks, Geneva Davis, Tracy Neal, Brandon McNeil, Lena & Keith Snowden, Clara Power, Lisa A. Smith, Donna Hailey, Shania Hayden, Corey Marshall, Doreen Smith, Tony McAuthor, Yvonne Lowe, Ronald Lowe, Yvette Revanales, Yvette aka Angie, Stuart Cinema & Cafe.

To my church family, The Starlight COGIC. Thank you for what you do!

The Robert Prince Washington Memorial District. I so appreciate you all!

Mt. Horeb Baptist Church family I appreciate and love you all!

If I bypassed anyone please put your name right here_____. I got you on the sequel!

Peace & Love,

BAR

Chapter 1

Anthony stood about 10 feet away from everyone else, in front of the T.V. in the yard of a maximum facility in upstate New York. Normally, Anthony wouldn't have been out in the yard, but tonight he had phone calls to make… and that required him to come out. BET was playing Monica's latest video "So Gone", and Anthony wanted more than anything to be so gone from this place it wasn't even funny. He reminded himself that his time was approaching, it just wasn't fast enough. As he finished making his calls, he was hoping the C.O.'s would call for an early go back, but they didn't. So, Anthony went back to watching BET.

Today, the Bloods had the T.V. on lock. And there they were, crowded around it, trying to catch glimpses of Monica's body. "Yo son, Monica's ass got fatter" shouted Brazy J, one of the Blood's front crew men here at the facility. He was a short stocky dude with a crazy looking afro. Some of the other guys agreed with him; Monica had definitely gained a few pounds in all the right places. Anthony chuckled in agreement, and found himself thinking lustful thoughts and quickly repented … for lust was not an easy demon to shake.

As Anthony stood staring at the T.V., he began thinking about what it would be like returning to society- and the many challenges that await him. His thoughts were interrupted when he heard someone in the back yell "Yo shorty!" Anthony didn't bother to turn around, because he knew whoever was calling for "shorty", certainly wasn't referring to him. Now, Anthony was about 5'8, and about a buck eighty-five, so he wasn't the biggest dude in the joint… but he sure as hell wasn't the smallest. If this was ten years ago, when he first entered the system, then maybe… but not now!

By this time, Monica's video had gone off and a new joint by Joe Budden was bumpin' from the T.V., when someone tapped Anthony on the shoulder. He turned around to see a dude that looked just like Iverson. He stood about 6'4, no shirt on, and sweating like he just completed a prison marathon or something. "Yo, you didn't hear me calling you, Shorty?" said Iverson, who actually went by the handle Preme. Preme had only been in this facility about a hot three weeks, but he was known by everybody who claimed to be somebody. Word had it that he had Harlem on lock, when it came to drugs. They say that anyone who is slinging around there is on his payroll… and that he has a slew of businesses; ranging from barber shops to designer boutiques.

"I heard someone calling shorty, but shorty ain't my handle." Anthony replied, knowing damn well where this could possibly lead to. "God help me" Anthony prayed inwardly. "My bad playa. I didn't know your name. And you are shorter than me… I wasn't trying to offend." Preme stated, as he stood towering over Anthony, with a pleading smile revealing nothing but platinum & diamonds. "No problem, no offense taken" Anthony said as he began upwardly praying that the early go back would be called… like now!

"So, what's your name, being that it ain't shorty?

"It's Ant."

"Okay Ant, I'm Preme." He extended his fist to give Ant some dap. "You look mad familiar. Where you from?" And wished he had a dollar for every time he heard someone say that to him… he'd be filthy rich.

"Jamaica Queens" Ant said. Preme smiled even bigger, showing dimples on both cheeks. "You know Fiddy (meaning 50 Cent, the newest rap phenomenon to come out of Queens since LL Cool J)?" asked Preme. Ant took a deep breath, preparing himself for the mental and spiritual battle he could sense brewing.

"I've seen him a few times at the Coliseum, but I don't know him" Ant said.

"That's my dawg; he comes and buys gear at one of my shops uptown. Have you seen his new video?"

"Nah I don't have a T.V., and I don't come outside unless I have to make phone calls... like tonight."

"You don't have a T.V. in that boring ass cell; how do you do it?" Ant said with a look of shock on his face.

"I read a lot" replied Ant.

"Damn, I hear that. So, what's up, you don't have the dough to buy one?" Asked Preme with a slight chuckle.

"I could swing it if I starved about a month, which I'm not willing to do. Plus, I'm trying to spend my time wisely" said Ant.

"I'm surprised no one up in this spot offered to buy you one." Preme said, with a slight grin, as he looked Ant up and down. Ant was so [inwardly] shaken by the way this conversation was starting to go, that he thought he would piss himself.

"Why would anyone offer to buy me a T.V.?" Asked Ant, while looking straight at Preme, with a look of displeasure. Preme still had that grin/smile plastered on his face, but he must've noticed Ant's displeasure, so he chose his response carefully.

"Look, I want us to be friends, so I don't want to say anything that will offend you… ya feel me? However, if you'll allow me to explain without you getting upset, I'll do my best." Right then, Ant's prayers were answered, and the announcement was made, that early go back would be in five minutes.

"As much as I would like to hear this (he was lying), I'm 'bout to head in, so if you can't explain it in five minutes, I'll have to catch you later." Ant knew damn well, the next time he'd be out would be in two weeks, when it was time to make his calls again.

"You're really going in early? What's so important in that cell, that you just have to go in?" Before Ant could respond, Preme kept on throwing out questions. "Why don't you just hang out? It'll only be an hour before everyone has to go in. It's a nice night, and I would really like to kick it with you." As much as Ant hated being in the yard, there was a part of him that actually wanted to stay and kick it with Preme.

"I told you, I have some reading to do, plus I have a few letters to write." Ant replied, hoping he sounded convincing enough. "That's bullshit, you don't have no letters to write, you just made phone calls, and your books ain't goin' nowhere; just chill for the hour shorty… I mean Ant. Just give me an hour. I promise you won't regret it."

"On the real, I need to go in, but I'll come out soon."

"When?" Asked Preme, not trying to hide his disappointment at all.

"Soon. Maybe over the weekend."

"Today is Monday! So, I gotta wait all the way until the weekend to kick it with you?" Before Ant could respond,

Preme said: "Alright, this weekend. And I'm gonna hold you to that."

Ant had not promised that he'd come out over the weekend, he had said maybe… but he didn't want to argue, and they were already beginning to line up for the early go back. Preme stuck out his hand for Ant to shake it, and said: "I'll see you Saturday night."

"Saturday." Ant said while shaking his hand. Preme, held onto Ant's hand a little longer than expected, and looked him in the eyes… as if he was trying to see through him. When Preme released his hand, Ant turned and headed towards the early go back lines. When he was about ten feet from where Preme had been standing, he heard Preme call him, so he stopped and turned around.

"Yo Ant, what's your last name?"

"Morgan. Why?"

"Just wanted to know."

With that, Ant stepped off, relieved to be going inside. Ant was always at ease when he was alone, but when he was forced to interact with strangers, that ease quickly vanished. It wasn't so much that Ant was uneasy talking with Preme, it was the fact that he found it relatively easy to talk with him… and that alone, made Ant uncomfortable.

The best thing, Ant concluded, was to go in and forget this entire evening; he had a Janet Evonovich novel waiting in his cell to be finished.

<u>Chapter 2</u>

Ant woke up early Thursday morning, sat up in his bed, and looked at the cell bars. Even after ten years of being locked up, he still thought he'd wake up and find that this was all a horrible nightmare… but it wasn't. So, like every morning, Ant got down on his knees to thank the Lord for another day. Despite his situation, God was still good to him, and he spent at least an hour in prayer every morning and every night before he went to bed.

Ant was a porter on the gallery he was housed in. His daily duties were to sweep and mop the gallery, clean the showers, give out supplies and meals to the "Keep-locks" (also known as the inmates in solitary), so Ant never had to go to the mess hall… and that was just fine with him. As he was getting himself together to start the days tasks, he thought of what excuse he could possibly give Preme for not showing up on Saturday; without lying. Ant hated liars; he was brought up to believe that liars were worse than thieves! Plus, he suffered enough at the hands of a liar, but he didn't want to think about that, nor the Preme situation. Instead, Ant thought about what book he would start reading today. He had just finished Patti LaBelle's autobiography, and he enjoyed it beyond measure. So he figured he'd start a good novel. Just then, his cell door opened and Ant stepped out, with his mind ready to work. As he headed to where the supplies were kept, the C.O. called him.

"Morgan, package room. Then go to the basement for a T.V. pick up."

"You sure it was me? I'm not expecting a package, nor did I order a T.V."

"Yeah, I'm sure it's you. I don't make mistakes. Go check it out" said Simmons, who was the steady officer on the gallery. He was cool in the sense that he didn't bother anyone, and he seemed to just want to do his eight hours and go home. Simmons gave Ant a pass and unlocked the gate to let him off the gallery. Then he said to Ant "You never know, maybe the man upstairs decided to lay it on someone's heart to bless you."

If that was the case, Ant couldn't figure out who it could be! He was just on the phone with his "family" Monday, and they never mentioned a package, let alone a T.V. As he approached the package room, Ant knew it had to be a mix up and that he would end up going back to the gallery empty handed. When he finally reached the package room, there was only one dude at the window, so he had to stand in line and wait his turn. Finally, the C.O. signaled for him to approach the window, in which he did, and handed the officer his pass and I.D card. The officer took it, left the window and returned a few seconds later with three huge buckets.

"You have thirty-five pounds of food, sixteen bars of soap, three deodorants, four hooded sweat suits, twelve pairs of socks, twenty boxer briefs and two pairs of Timberland boots."

Ant was in total shock, and for a few seconds, he couldn't speak. "Are you sure this stuff is for me?" Ant asked, finally able to speak.

"You're Morgan alright" the officer said, looking from the photo on the I.D. card to Ant.

"Yea but…"

"The stuff came in today for you, so take it. I hope you ate your Wheaties this morning; cause this shit is heavy."

ChoirBoy

****

It was just after noon and Ant had completed all his morning tasks: sweeping, mopping, feeding all the keep-locks and disposing of their garbage. Ant's next-door neighbor was moving shortly to the annex part of the jail, and Ant had to help him, cause the brother had more bags than one man could handle. The annex was a good twenty-minute walk and Ant did not look forward to it... but he was used to doing things he didn't want to do.

Ant's mind was more focused on trying to figure out who had sent him the boots, clothes, food and a T.V. It bothered him so bad, that he went to Officer Simmons and asked if he could use the phone on the gallery. For some reason, the jail didn't want inmates using the phones on the gallery, they wanted them to make all their calls outside or in the gym. Some of the C.O.'s didn't really mind. Simmons granted Ant's request for two reasons; Ant never asked for any favors and he was never a problem. Secondly, Ant was the best worker Simmons ever had. Also, Simmons sensed Ant's bewilderment concerning this morning's events.

Ant called everyone he could think of, only to find that no one he knew had sent him the stuff. Ant knew that sooner or later he would find out... he was hoping more sooner than later.

****

Ant was making his way back from helping his neighbor move to the annex. It had taken a little longer than he expected, because he had to stop a couple of times and re-adjust the heavy bags. As he approached the gallery, he had his mind set to take a quick shower and watch some T.V., until it was time to do the dinner feed-up. As he got on the gallery, C.O. Simmons was preparing to go home for the day.

"You got a new neighbor while you were gone. Ain't been here but a couple of weeks and has more shit than I do at home. Don't even know how all that shit got in the cell" Simmons stated when Ant reached him.

"Hopefully he's quiet" Ant replied.

"Alright, lock in until the next shift gets here... I'll see you in the morning."

Ant went down to his cell and stepped in, seconds before the gate closed and locked. He sat down on the bed and turned on his new 13" color T.V., and began surfing channels. Ant settled on a movie called "The Best Man", which was just starting on HBO. He had just settled back on the bed when there was a tap on the wall. Ant hadn't met his new neighbor to the left of him, in which the knocking was coming from.

"Yo what's happening?" Ant asked.

"Yo, do you have a mirror I can borrow for a second, I can't find mine in all this junk." The neighbor said.

"Give me a second." As Ant went to grab his mirror from over the sink, he tried to place the voice of his new neighbor. The voice sounded familiar, but not one he could place. Ant got the mirror, and stuck his arm out of the gate so his new neighbor could grab it.

"Good lookin'." Said the voice, as Ant went and laid back on his bed, in front of the T.V.

Chapter 3

Friday had come and gone with a blur. Nothing of importance had transpired, and Ant still had not met his new neighbor. Ant had fallen asleep Thursday night while watching a romantic comedy. He had awakened early Friday morning to find the mirror he had lent to his mysterious neighbor on his cell bars.

Every time Ant was out and about, his neighbors cell bars were always covered with a sheet. Normally a dude only put the sheet up for one of two reasons: 1- because he's using the bathroom (which includes taking a "bird bath" in the sink) or 2- he was jerking off to paper bitches. Whatever the reason, this dude keeping the sheet up was alright with Ant. What was also alright, was the fact that he hadn't spoken to Ant since requesting the mirror. Ant didn't believe in talking on the gate, so whoever this dude was, he was the ideal neighbor.

****

It was Saturday, and as Ant gave the keep-locks their dinner, he thought of Preme and how he would be expecting him in the yard tonight. Ant knew he wasn't going, but what would be his excuse when he saw Preme again? Ant knew he couldn't stay up on the gallery forever.

After everyone had eaten and the garbage had been disposed of, Ant was back in his cell in front of the T.V. when the C.O. came around asking who was going to the yard. It seemed like everyone was going out, with the exception of the three keep-locks up front.

"Yard Morgan?" The C.O. asked when he reached Ant's cell.

"No, not tonight."

"You're gonna stay in on a nice night like tonight? So far, you'll be the only one up here, other than those three assholes up front. I'll keep your cell, the slop sink and the shower open and I'll lock you in when everyone is coming back from the yard."

"Alright. Thanks."

The C.O. stepped over to the next cell and asked the unknown person was he going to the yard.

"No, I'm good."

"Morgan, you've got company tonight." Said the officer, as he made his way back off the gallery.

Ant sat there watching T.V. and had no idea as to what he was watching. Moments passed and finally the cell gates opened. Everyone made a mad dash off the gallery in pursuit to be at the head of the line in route to the yard. When the C.O. closed the cells, Ant came out of his cell and went to the showers. While he was in the shower, he thought of the T.V., and the new gear he had received this week. With still no clue as to where the stuff came from, he was grateful for it, as long as there were no unwanted surprises that would come along later.

Twenty minutes later, he got out of the shower and made his way down to his cell. After he finished grooming, he decided to put on one of the new sweat suits and a pair of the Timbs. Ant wasn't going anywhere, but he figured what's the point of having the stuff and just letting it lay there. After he had gotten dressed, he looked in the mirror and liked the Anthony Morgan he saw. Just then, there was a tap on the wall from Ant's unknown neighbor.

ChoirBoy

"Yo what's up?" Ant asked.

"Could you bring me a bucket of hot water?"

"Sure, give me a sec." Ant came out of his cell and went to the slop sink to fill a bucket of water. He took the bucket of water to his neighbor's cell, which was still covered with the sheet tied to the bars. On the floor inside the cell, sat a white-water pail. Ant bent down, placed the spout of the water bucket between the bars, just over the empty pail and began pouring. As he was pouring the water, a voice came from behind the curtain.

"That's real fucked up that you had no intentions on keeping your word tonight."

Before Ant could mentally digest what was just stated, the sheet that was once tied to the bars had been snatched away. When Ant looked up, he was staring into the glaring eyes of Preme. Ant was so caught off guard, that he hadn't realized he had filled the bucket. Before Ant could respond, Preme kept going, using Ant's shock to his advantage.

"Then I move in here on Thursday and you don't even have the decency to check on a brother and see if he's alright or needs anything. What kind of neighbor are you? By the way, I'm feeling the suit and the Timbs. That's real foul shorty."

"I told you it's…"

"Yea, yea, I know. It's Ant."

"And for the record…"

"Yeah, I know what you're gonna say. That you never promised to come out. But when I said 'I'll see you Saturday', your reply was Saturday." By this time, Ant had stood up and was standing in front of Preme with this "jackass" look on his face, from having been busted. Ant looked up and saw Preme standing there, arms folded, wearing a wife beater and baggy cargo shorts.

"You just gonna stand there and not say anything?" Preme continued to stand there glaring, waiting for a response.

"I didn't know it was you who moved in; every single time I came pass; you had the sheet up."

"Regardless of the fact that you didn't know it was me, you couldn't show no hospitality, and make sure your new neighbor was alright? I could have been dead in here and you wouldn't have known it or cared. Plus, that doesn't change the fact that you stood me up tonight."

"You're right, I'm not even going to try and justify that; I apologize."

"What the fuck is your problem? A brother tries to be nice to you and you get on some real bullshit." By this time, Ant could no longer look Preme in the face. Ant was feeling guilty for having mislead Preme about coming out tonight and for not checking on his neighbor. It irked Ant that Preme could make him feel like he had just robbed a town bank and left the entire community nothing. Ant knew he couldn't stand there with the "jackass" face all night; he had to say something. It was time to be honest.

"Alright, I was just a bit uncomfortable with how you befriended me. Then there was a question in my mind... why me? Out of the 2100 inmates in this joint, why me? And Lastly, you held my hand just a bit too long when you shook it."

"Wait a minute. Don't tell me you think I want to fuck you?" Preme stood, leaning on the bars waiting for an answer. Seconds passed and Ant had yet to reply, so Preme pressed on. "You might as well continue to keep it real." Ant thought to himself, that he's right, he might as well keep it real; in for a penny, in for a pound.

"I'm not saying that was your motive, but it all just felt funny, especially you calling me shorty and all." Ant hoped he had worded his response correctly, and that Preme would not take more offense and flip. Just then, Preme began to chuckle. "You pretty boys are all the same; y'all think that every fuckin body wants you."

Ant had long ago come to terms with his looks. It was not easy admitting that both men and women found him attractive. His caramel colored skin, his naturally curly jet-black hair and his hazel eyes made most people do a double take. However, Ant was not used to being called a pretty boy. For personal reasons, since his childhood, he always tried to down play his looks, all to no avail.

Ant began to think that he had misjudged Preme, and that maybe his childhood had robbed him of all rational thinking and the ability to be a judge of character. Ant couldn't move, nor could he hold his emotions in check any longer, as a single tear fell from each of his eyes. Preme saw the tears fall from Ant's eyes and thought maybe he pushed too hard. Preme also sensed that there was so much more to Ant than meets the eye. He took a deep breath and began speaking.

"Look, I didn't mean to come across so abrupt. I just get hyped from time to time. I don't know you, but I was just trying to be friendly. Based on what I've been told, you've been down for a minute, for a crazy injustice, which no one seems to know details on. You keep to yourself in here, so it's obvious to me that you've had it rough. I don't sex dudes; I gets way too much pussy for that. I, for some strange reason, just wanted to be a friend and help. That's why I had the T.V. and other stuff sent to you."

"You sent that stuff?" Ant asked, with a look of disbelief & shock plastered on his face.

"Who do you think sent it to you? That's why I asked for your last name, and before you start again, there are no strings attached. I have more money than I know what to do with, so don't even get phased by that little bit of bullshit. I could do that for every cat in this joint, and still not be broke... believe that."

Ant's emotions were going in complete havoc. Could it be true? Someone actually had a sincere, genuine interest in him, with no strings attached? And a male at that! Or, was this a set up? Sure, there are some older women he's met while being locked up, that come into the facilities to have church, and they've "adopted" him and have become like family to him. Ant knows that those sisters knew who he was, and how "real" family turned their backs on him, some ten years ago. But, could someone like Preme just care about him to be caring? Ant shook his head, and the tears really began to flow.

"Ant, talk to me, what's going on? You have my word it won't go any further, and I promise to do what I can to help you."

Preme was shaken by Ant's loss of composure and his heart went out to the kid. "Come on Ant... talk to me."

Ant couldn't find his voice and just continued shaking his head from side to side, as tears flowed and covered his face. Just then, the C.O. yelled from the front of the gallery; "Morgan, take it in. Yards coming in." Ant ran into his cell and as the gate closed, Ant fell on his bed in a heap of uncontrolled sobs.

****

Two hours later, the gallery was dark and quiet. The C.O. had already taken his count and Ant was still laying on his bed, and the only light was coming from his muted T.V. As if on cue, Preme stuck his mirror over to look in Ant's cell, and when Ant looked up, he asked:

"You iight?"

"I will be" Ant replied.

"Come sit by the bars, so we don't have to talk loud." Ant sat up and slid down to the foot of the bed and rested his arms on the bars. Preme got comfortable on a stool and continued to hold the mirror, so they could see each other.

"Ant, I can't help you if I don't know the situation. Furthermore, you can't help yourself unless you're willing to talk about it. Talking about it not only lightens your load and makes you feel better, but it starts the healing process as well. Trust me, I speak from experience." Ant thought about what Preme had stated and there was something within, telling him that Preme was right; he needed to get it out and he needed to heal.

"Ant trust me on this one. Take your time, and give it to me from the beginning." Ant wiped his face with his hand, took a deep breath and slowly began speaking.

"It's a long, long story, but it started when…"

<u>Chapter 4</u>

"**H**old still, I'm almost there. Stop all that damn noise. Oh, oh, here I go." Said Shadrack (The Reverend Shadrack E. Brown, pastor of The Greater Second Chance Love Revival Tabernacle), who fell exhaustedly onto the little body that laid beneath him. Finally, Shadrack slowly pulled his 327-pound fat ass up from bed, and planted his wobbly legs on the floor. Anthony Morgan, Shadrack's step-son, laid on the bed motionless, in pain and wishing he was dead. Even now, at 11 years-old after four years of Shadrack's violations, he could never get used to the torment; every time was just as bad as the first time.

"Get up boy and get ya loose asshole having ass in the shower, your momma will be here in an hour, and we need to be ready to leave for service when she gets in. Anthony rolled over, got up from the bed and put his pants & underwear back on.

"What the hell you been doing? That ass used to be tight as hell! Now, I get about the same kinda ride out of you and ya momma! I thought if I stayed off you for a few weeks, when I came back, it would be tight again!" Anthony, despite how hurt he was physically & mentally, knew better than to say anything, because he knew Shadrack would go off on him; he just remained quiet.

"And don't go singing that damn Timothy Wright song 'Jesus Will' or that 'I won't complain'. I know you're hoping that Jesus will get rid of me, but that ain't gonna happen. Just keep your damn mouth shut about our business, and you'll be alright. With that being said, you don't have anything to complain about anyway, so sing something happy and joyful… that always helps me to preach better. You hear me boy?"

"Yes sir." Anthony replied, as he turned in the direction of his bedroom. Then Shadrack spoke again. "And another thing, get into some trouble sometimes; all boys get into mischief. Chase some of the little girls at the church, squeeze some ass and titties, that's always a plus. You don't do shit! You don't chase girls, you don't play sports, you don't do a damn thing. Nothing! You make me sick!" Anthony stood there thinking how foolish he sounded. How could he do those things when every day after school and on Saturdays, he has to clean the church and practice the organ? But Anthony dare not remind him of all that.

"What the fuck you still standing there for? I told your silly ass we gotta be ready to leave as soon as your momma gets here! Now go!" Anthony quickly left Shadrack and his mother's bedroom and went to his. He sat down on the bed and began to crying. All he could think of was why his dad had to die [when he was three]. If his father had still been alive, his mother would've never married Shadrack, and he wouldn't have been subjected to Shadrack's deranged sexual appetite. Shadrack had started abusing Anthony at the age of seven. He "took" Anthony, whenever they were alone. If they were home and his mom was out shopping or at the church, if they were alone at the church, and sometimes late at night while his wife was asleep. At the very beginning, the abuse would occur 3-4 times a week. Lately, he would go so long without hurting him, that Anthony thought maybe Shadrack had lost interest. But every time Anthony got that impression, Shadrack's fat ass would start creeping again.

Anthony began getting himself together so he could be ready when Shadrack and his mom were ready to leave for service. As usual, he began moving about, working on autopilot. He had learned to distract himself from his feelings & emotions. When Shadrack first started the abuse, Anthony thought it was his fault and was plagued with guilt. Then he realized, after some time, that it was Shadrack who had the problem. Anthony couldn't help but feel like people could see his hurt and the fact that he was being abused. He worked diligently to keep the madness hidden from everyone. Unfortunately, he didn't have to work very hard at all.

Anthony couldn't keep his eyes or mind off the female body. In school, the girls both loved and feared him, for he was known to flash his 11-year-old penis at them from time to time. He'd walk into the girl's locker room when they were changing, and attempt to stick his tongue in their mouths! The strange thing is, they would never tell on him… to the adults; he was the perfect little gentleman! Anthony had also discovered porn and masturbation. Shadrack had lots of XXX Rated videos stashed away, that Anthony would watch any time he was alone. Hidden under his mattress, was photos taken from *Playboy*, *Penthouse* & *Hustler*, that he and the other boys could get their hands on.

As Anthony finished getting dressed, he thought of how much he hated Shadrack, and how much he hated hearing him preach. He'd be in the pulpit, yelling and screaming about sin and hell fire… and he was the biggest sinner of them all! Anthony couldn't figure out what his mother saw in his fat, disgusting, ugly ass. Actually, several women at the church would talk about how handsome Shadrack is, how good he preached and sang. But he was fat and nasty, and would run to the bathroom ten minutes after he ate a meal!

One would conclude that Sylvia (Anthony's mom), saw an opportunity in Shadrack. He was a single 45-year-old, charismatic preacher on the rise, with a few dollars in his pockets. Sylvia was a 43-year-old widow with a 5-year-old son, working a job as a secretary, and was still sexy as hell. Many in Sylvia's shoes probably would've done the same thing. There was also that possibility that Sylvia really did love Shadrack. She was always supportive of him (too supportive if you asked Anthony), always cooked, kept the house clean and always looked good whenever she stepped out. Shadrack would always boast to the deacons, trustees and other ministers, how his wife kept it goin' on.

The only problem Anthony had with his mother was that she couldn't see the dog that Shadrack really was! She couldn't see the pain he was inflicting on her **ONLY** child. Despite all of that, Anthony still loved his mom with all his heart, and prayed daily that she would leave Shadrack. It also troubled Anthony, that his mom didn't know Shadrack's complete background. All she knew was that he was born in Florida, parents were deceased, no siblings and he was married once before. Shadrack claimed that he came from a week long revival in Poon Creek, Georgia, to find his pregnant wife gone, with all of their savings. The only time he had heard from her was when the divorce was finalized. Eighteen months after the divorce he met Sylvia, and six months later they were married.

****

That evening in service Anthony sat behind the black baby grand piano (he didn't have the confidence to play the Hammond B-3 organ, so he left that to the more experienced musicians), dazed and not really aware of what was happening in the service. When Shadrack went to the podium, Anthony prayed that he wouldn't call on him.

"My brothers & my beautiful sisters" Shadrack began. "The Lord has given me a sermon for you all tonight titled "Where is Your Head". Why don't you turn to your neighbor and ask them- *Neighbor, where is your head?* Now sisters, if you're sitting next to a brother, ask them again without being fresh." Shadrack laughed his sick, triflin' laugh, as did some of the congregants. Shadrack could call them a bunch of dumb assholes, and they would probably laugh and say "Amen pastor." "But, before I break the bread, I'm gonna call my boy, Professor Anthony, to bless us with a song of his choosing." Anthony got up from the piano and made his way to the center of the pulpit where Shadrack was standing, waiting to give him the microphone.

When Anthony reached the center, Shadrack handed him the mic. But before he turned it loose, he bent over slightly and whispered in Anthony's ear "Remember what I said boy". Anthony took the mic, stood there for a few minutes with his head down, trying to keep his emotions in check. Finally, he opened his mouth and the voice that thundered through the church was too mature to be coming from an 11-year-old. There were adults three times Anthony's age who didn't have the range and vocal control that he possessed. Every time he sang, the congregants would be captivated by the song.

"Faith that Conquers Anything" was the song Anthony sang, as the congregants stood on their feet and yelled for him to sing. The more he sang about that faith that could conquer anything, the spirit moved on him like never before. Tears began to fall from his eyes as he riffed and belted out notes that would've made Vanessa Bell Armstrong never sing her song again; had she heard Anthony signing that night! As Anthony proceeded towards the end of the song, the congregation was on their feet, yelling, praising & worshipping God and speaking in tongues. When the final note was hit, a praise went forth. People began dancing and some were slain in the spirit.

With a tear stained face, Anthony made his way back to the piano. While in route, the church Mother [Mother Green] made her way over to Anthony. When she reached him, she laid her 84-year-old hand on Anthony's forehead. This lone gesture caused Anthony to break down into uncontrollable sobs. Mother Green bent down and whispered in Anthony's ear:

"The Lord said He is with you and He will bring you through. He said to tell you He sees you and He cares. He has not forgotten you. I am with you, saith the Lord."

Mother Green touched Anthony's forehead once again with her palm. It was then that Anthony hit the floor in a faint.

Later that night while lying in his bed, Anthony experienced a peace that he had never felt in his entire life. He didn't know how, but he knew one day his situation would be over!

Chapter 5

Since that night several months ago, when Mother Green had laid hands on Anthony and told him what the Lord had said, they had become inseparable. Every day after school Mother Green would keep Anthony company as he practiced the organ and cleaned the church. Anthony cherished and lived for his time special time with Mother Green. She was the only bright spot in his life. She would bake all of Anthony's favorite desserts and tell him lots of stories.

Mother Green knew in her heart that there was something seriously troubling Anthony, but she never tried to force it out of him. Instead, she prayed for him diligently, encouraged him and showed him as much love as she possibly could. Anthony could tell that Mother Green suspected something, and he loved the fact that she never tried to pry and force it out of him. He knew she would wait until he was good and ready to talk about it, but Anthony wasn't ready… he didn't know if he'd ever be.

One afternoon, a week before his 12th birthday, Anthony walked to church from school with purpose in each step. The night before, Shadrack brought his nasty, fat, trifling, disgusting ass into Anthony's bedroom while Sylvia was sleep, and violated him. Anthony was sick and tired of it and had made up in his mind to tell Mother Green and seek her help. When Anthony got to the church, Mother Green wasn't there waiting. This was not unusual, sometimes she would get caught up in prayer, talking on the phone or baking, that she would lose track of time. Anthony let himself into the church and began his routine. Two hours later, Mother Green hadn't showed up and as Anthony locked the church, he made up in his mind that he wouldn't lose heart, he would tell Mother Green about Shadrack tomorrow.

Anthony made his way home and when he was several yards from the house, a creepy feeling fell over him. Then he noticed several cars belonging to some of the church members parked on the block. Anthony figured that there was some sort of church meeting taking place; Shadrack and his mom never informed him of the happenings, so everything was a surprise to him. As soon as Anthony stepped foot in the house, he knew it wasn't a church meeting taking place. He looked around and saw Shadrack, several of the ministers, deacons and church members, but he didn't see Sylvia. Immediately his heart began to race, as he stood in the entrance; unable to move. Suddenly, Shadrack got up and made his way over to where Anthony was stuck standing. Anthony was just about to lose it, but just as Shadrack got over to him, Sylvia stepped out of the kitchen wiping her hands on a towel. Everyone in the house got so quiet, you could've heard a roach pee on a cotton (not that there were roaches in Shadrack's house, no sir. If he saw one, he'd have someone's ass, yes pun intended). Shadrack placed his hand on Anthony's shoulder, looked him in the face and slowly began talking.

"Son, I have some bad news for you. Before I tell you, I want you to know, the Lord doesn't make mistakes." The members that were packed in the house began shaking their heads in agreement, saying "Amen pastor." Shadrack continued, "The Lord said He giveth and He taketh away. This morning, the Lord knew what He was doing when He called our precious Mother Green home, to be with HIM. Son the Lord…" Shadrack continued, but Anthony didn't hear another word he said. Anthony wasn't even aware that tears were streaming down his face. He was vaguely aware that several of the church members made their way towards him and began hugging, touching and patting him on the head. Anthony pushed passed the adults and ran directly to his room. When he reached there, he stepped in, slammed the door and fell face first on his bed. By this time, tears were accompanied by sobs and moans of pure anguish. "Why God! Why now?" Anthony cried into his pillow. Anthony was taught at an early age to never ever question God, but this was just too much to bear! Sometime later, Anthony finally fell asleep, wishing he could be where Mother Green was. In Anthony's mind, there was no way he could go on living.

****

The week had passed by, it was all a blur to Anthony. Today was his 12th birthday and it was also the day of Mother Green's home going service and burial. One thing was for sure, birthdays would never be the same for Anthony ever again.

****

Anthony walked into the church behind Shadrack and Sylvia. That walk of purpose he had just a mere seven days ago, was now gone… with no hopes of ever returning. The church was so packed that there were people standing in the back and in the aisles. Shadrack had estimated that 250-300 people would attend the service today, and he wasn't far off. Anthony made his way down front to the piano, and as he made his way, he caught sight of several hundred floral arrangements, and there in the middle of all the flowers, sat a simple yet elegant open gold casket. With his heart pounding and tears flowing, he stepped in front of the casket and looked at Mother Green. She was laying there with a smile on her face, in a beautiful cream-colored dress. She looked as if she was taking a quick nap, like she often did between services on Sundays.

As Anthony stood there, not trying to hold in his emotions one bit, suddenly someone grabbed his shoulders, turned him around and hugged him. They hugged him like Mother Green used to. Before his mind could register what was happening, the person hugging him spoke. "It's alright son, we'll see her again someday." Anthony hugged Sylvia like it was his last time, little did he know… it would be.

****

Anthony braced himself as he listened to Shadrack introduce him: "Yes Mother Green loved him as much as I do, if that's possible. She loved to hear him sing and even if he wasn't scheduled to sing, she would make a special request. This celebration would not be complete without having him bless us with a selection. Anthony" Anthony got up from the piano and made his way to the center of the podium [right behind the casket] and took the mic from Shadrack. Anthony gave the musicians and the choir a nod that he was ready. The music began and the 66-member choir stood and began to sway, as Anthony began to sing.

"If anybody asks you where I'm going… I'm going up yonder to be with my Lord." The spirit had to be on Anthony, for he sung as if he discovered his voice for the very first time. Tears streamed down his face, as he continued to belt out note after note, as he walked back and forth across the stage. The members of Greater Second Chance Love Revival Tabernacle had never seen Anthony sing like this before. There wasn't a dry eye in the place, nor was anyone still seated. Mother Green's six children, twenty-four grandchildren and thirteen great-grandchildren were all in the first two pews, and each one was crying. Shouts of joy, praise and sorrow came from every corner of the church. Anthony, was unaware of the near chaotic congregants. Despite his roller-coaster of emotions, he knew he had to sing this song for his only true friend, who was now gone.

****

After the burial, the family and the church members all went back to the church where a big feast was prepared. There was so much food that they could've fed everyone that was shopping on Jamaica Ave, and there would still be food left. Anthony wasn't hungry, so he sat alone in the church and played softly on the organ. A voice came from behind him. Anthony didn't know who it was, nor did he really care. "She told me you could sing and play, but I wasn't prepared for what I heard from you today." Anthony looked up and the voice that was talking to him was standing right next to him. He recognized the man as being Mother Green's oldest son Harold.

"She spoke of me?" asked Anthony. "Every time I spoke to her, she would tell me what a remarkable, gifted and loving young man you are. She would say "I hope he marries one of my grands. She loved you very, very much." Touched by the words, Anthony wiped his eyes. Harold continued… "When we were going through some of her things at the house, we came across something that had your name on it. Then we found a list of instructions and in it, she requested that we make sure you got it." Harold's hand came from behind his back and produced Mother Green's worn and battered black leather Bible. On top of the Bible was a plain white envelope with Mother Green's handwriting, that simply said "Master Anthony" on it.

ChoirBoy

Anthony took the Bible and the envelope from Harold and stared at it.

Harold took a seat on the organ bench next to Anthony. He reached inside his jacket pocket and produced a business card, which he handed to Anthony. "I don't know what you're going through, but mama said that underneath you are troubled. She loved you very much and because she did, so do I. If you ever need me, here is my home, office and pager numbers; call me. It makes no difference what time… just call. Houston, Texas isn't that far away." Harold placed an arm around him and pulled him close. After a few minutes, he released him and stood up. "I'll leave you for now. Take care "Master Anthony". And don't forget, you're not alone. Call whenever you're ready." Harold turned and headed toward the exit that would lead back to the dining area, when Anthony yelled out: "Harold… I'll call one day!" Harold nodded and left Anthony alone, still holding the Bible and Envelope.

Slowly, Anthony placed the Bible on the organ and stared at the envelope. Very carefully he opened it. Enclosed, were two hand written pages; he began reading.

Dearest Master Anthony,

If you are reading this letter, it must mean two things: 1- I've gone on home to be with the Lord and 2- My children finally did something I told them (smile). Do not be sad about my passing. I've lived 80 plus years, longing for the day I can be in Heaven with the King of Kings and Lord of Lords! Just picture me up here in my big ole mansion whenever you feel sad and lonely about me being gone.

The Lord had shown me that night you sang about Faith, that you were burdened and troubled far beyond your years. But the Lord gave you a promise that He would be with you always. He has a plan and purpose for your life, far greater than you could ever imagine. It may not seem like it now, but trust the word that the Lord has spoken through me.

I've never pressed you about what's going on in your life, but I figure it has to do with your momma's lack of interest in you, and I strongly believe the core of it all is that Rev. Shadrack E. Brown. He's a jack leg preacher, if I ever saw one. I had often asked the Lord why He still had me there, even after He showed me Shadrack was no good. The spirit would always tell me that I would understand it better by and by. Anthony, the Lord kept me there for you. Now that I'm gone, don't think for a second that you can't make it. The Lord does not make mistakes and He won't put more on you than you can bare.

Know that I've loved you as if you were one of my very own. Stay in the word and always pray. God is going to bring you through it and use you mightily. Be everything Shadrack is not! Finally, my child, be strong in the Lord and in the power of HIS might!

With all my heart and love,
Mother Green

Anthony refolded the letter, placed it back in the envelope and into his jacket pocket. He wiped his eyes and thought of a place he could hide the letter so Shadrack wouldn't find it. Just then, he saw Harold and his family heading through the exit doors. Anthony jumped off the organ and ran towards them. When he was still a few feet away, he called out "Harold." Harold turned around and saw Anthony headed in his direction. He said something to his family, and then made his way towards Anthony. When they reached each other, Anthony handed him the envelope.

"Please keep this for me, I will come for it later. Right now, I don't have a safe place to keep it." "No problem lil' brother. I'll have it when you're ready for it." Harold held out his hand for Anthony to shake it, and before Anthony knew it, he had thrown his arms around Harold. Harold was a bit surprised, but didn't show it. As Harold held him, he whispered in his ear "Everyone is not him. Call me when you're ready to talk."

Chapter 6

The months that followed Mother Green's passing went by, all while Anthony was in a functional haze of pure agony. He still continued straight A's in school, continued to wow churches all over the Tri-State area with his soaring vocals, as well as playing the piano. What also continued, was Shadrack's late night creeps, along with Anthony's lust for women, pornography and masturbation.

In the months after Mother Green's passing, things had really changed at the church as well. Several families who had been so faithful and diligent, had left the church to worship elsewhere. This had stressed Shadrack to degrees beyond belief. Nothing anyone said or did seemed to please him. Even his once easy, carefree marriage to Sylvia seemed to be strained. The only joy Shadrack seemed to get, was when he was on top of Anthony.

Things had changed for everyone, one Sunday when Shadrack opened the doors of the church. A couple who had been attending for about three weeks, along with their two daughters, ages 15 and 11, made their way down to the front, where Shadrack was standing. This family was the first new members Greater Second Chance Love Revival Tabernacle had seen in God only knew how long. Shadrack and his faithful followers felt this was a sign that things were changing. And after receiving the Reed family, the entire church broke out into uncontrollable dancing. They hopped and ran around the church for at least an hour.

Anthony was on the organ playing, and he too felt something… and it surely wasn't the Holy Ghost. The Reed's oldest daughter was fine as hell. She was 4'11 about 100 lbs., and what the old timers would call a "redbone". She had wavy brown hair, that seemed to be the same color as her eyes, and it came down to the center of her back. There was a worldly song that Anthony had heard from time to time called "Brick House" ... the Reed girl was just that; a Brick House!

****

Four months later, and eight months after Mother Green's passing, Mr. & Mrs. Reed, along with their oldest daughter Renee, sat in Shadrack and Sylvia's living room with Anthony. This was not a social call, nor was it a prayer meeting. Mr. Reed spoke: "Pastor, there is no easy way to say this to you and First Lady Sylvia. Our daughter Renee, who just turned sixteen, is pregnant by your thirteen-year-old son."

****

Four months later, on the eve of his thirteenth birthday, Anthony was sitting in his honors English class, getting a jump start on his homework, when the teacher informed him that he was wanted in the principal's office. Anthony gathered his belongings and headed out, in route to see the principal. He was sure it was a warning about his two unexcused absences last week (in which he was taking care of a 14-year-old, brown skinned, high school freshman, with a fat ass). When Anthony got to the office, the secretary told him to go right in. She was not a member of Greater Second Chance Love Revival Tabernacle, but she had attended several funerals and weddings, so she knew who Anthony was. Plus, Anthony had sung at her church, First Church of God in Christ, several times.

When he swung open the door, he was shocked to see Shadrack and his mom sitting there. When Anthony entered, the principal, along with his mom and Shadrack, stood up. "Son, we have to go to the hospital, Renee had a miscarriage this morning."

****

The day after Renee's miscarriage, Mr. Reed asked his boss for a transfer. The transfer came through, and three weeks later, the entire Reed family left New York for a new life in Sioux Falls, South Dakota.

After the loss of his child and Renee moving, Anthony fell deeper and deeper into sexual mischief. Not only that, his whole attitude and demeanor began to change. Instead of just sitting at home, cleaning the church and practicing the organ, Anthony decided to apply for a part-time job at the Western Beef on Merrick Blvd. Anthony worked as much as possible, so he didn't have to be home… with Shadrack. Sylvia didn't seem to miss him, or care that he was often gone As long as she was able to buy her Dolce & Gabbana and Ferragamo stilettos, she was content. Shadrack bitched and complained about Anthony not being faithful to the ministry. Anthony's feelings on Shadrack bitching was simply; fuck him!

****

Anthony had been at Western Beef for a little over two years, and at the age of fifteen, he was the youngest part-time manager in the company's history. His hard work, diligence and maturity had won him the position, after being on the job a mere 11 months. In the time he had been working, Anthony was able to avoid being alone with Shadrack and that was better than getting a pay check each week. Despite his desire to fuck any female that looked halfway decent, Anthony was starting to feel good about himself. Even convinced himself that Shadrack had lost interest in him.

ChoirBoy

It was Friday, and Anthony had the entire weekend off. Adding icing to the cake, Shadrack and Sylvia were leaving for the night to go to attend a conference. So instead of heading to work, now that classes were over for the week, Anthony headed home to see the "love birds" off. When Anthony walked into the house, he saw two suitcases resting by the door. Anthony's mind quickly thought about the 19-year-old "redbone" with the fat ass, that he'd be hittin' doggy-style once Shadrack and Sylvia had cleared the Tri-State. Sylvia came flying out of the kitchen and saw Anthony standing there. She gave no greeting and just began talking a mile a minute. "Son, there's been a change of plans." Anthony got nervous, thinking they were going to make him go to D.C. as well. "There's a flood at the church and Shadrack is there now with the plumbers. It's a major valve and it's going to take some time to fix, so Shadrack won't be going with me to D.C.; he'll be here with you for the weekend."

Anthony couldn't believe what he was hearing. This couldn't be happening to him. "Oh, hell no! What the hell you mean he ain't going? Have him get his fat ass on a plane when he's finished at the church." Sylvia calmly walked over to Anthony and with all her might, she slapped the taste outta his mouth! "How dare you stand in my face, in my house and speak like that, especially about the man of God. Just because we treat you like your grown, doesn't mean you are! Now, I don't want to hear another word from you, unless it's an apology." Sylvia paused to see if Anthony would indeed apologize for his outburst. But when he didn't, she continued. "I'm not going to tell pastor about the horrible things you said tonight. It would break his heart!"

"He broke my heart, when he started creeping into my room when I was seven, and began riding me like he rides you… or does he even bother?" This was the first time Anthony had ever spoken of the torment Shadrack had been enforcing on him over the years. "Where were you when the "Man of God" was sticking his nasty dick all in my ass? Where the hell were you, when I was crying out for help?!" By this time, Anthony was both yelling and crying. Sylvia just stood there, unable to believe the filth that was coming out of this child's mouth. It had to be a demon that possessed him and it was now controlling him. She walked over to him and slapped his face a second time. "I rebuke that filthy, lying tongue of yours. I am going to pick up my bags and leave this house. Again, I am not going to break Shadrack's heart by telling him of your Oscar worthy performance today. When I return from D.C., I expect an apology, and that you have returned back to being the respectful young man that Shadrack and I raised."

Sylvia grabbed her bags and headed for the door. When she reached the door, she turned back to Anthony and said: "Have a blessed weekend." Anthony watched her walk out of the house, and the door slammed behind her. He couldn't believe she rejected the truth and took Shadrack's side over her own son's. Right then and there, Anthony made up in his mind that he was no longer going to run from Shadrack's nasty ass, nor was he going to be a victim any longer.

He raced to his bedroom, pulled the sheets off his bed, where in the middle of the mattress was a hole, which served two purposes. 1- From time to time, he would stick his prick in and hump until he got his nut, and 2- he hid his money that he made at Western Beef. He retrieved his money and turned to run out of the room. As he was about to exit, something on the dresser caught his eye. It was the little black Bible that Mother Green had given to him. Anthony stood there, transfixed by the sight of that most holy and sacred book. For a moment, he second guessed his decision… and just as quickly as the thought came, it left.

Anthony was out of the house in a flash. His destination was a place called "South Road", located in the slums of Jamaica, Queens, where anything could be bought for the right price.

****

At the same time that Anthony was leaving the house, Shadrack was locking up the church. The plumbers had left for the day, and would be back in the morning. Shadrack had planned on going straight home to Anthony, but as he was locking up, he received a page and was going to make a pit stop in Brooklyn. You see, Shadrack, Sylvia and Anthony always rocked the newest and hottest clothing; all courtesy of Shadrack. Everyone figured the Reverend just went from store to store, spending huge amounts of money to keep himself and his family looking good. However, that was not the case. Shadrack secretly bought stolen goods from a seventeen-year-old homosexual booster named Peaches, from the Fort Green projects of Brooklyn. This relationship between Peaches and Shadrack had been going on for well over two years, ever since Peaches started boosting.

Peaches would only charge Shadrack 35% of what the garments actually costed. Peaches did this for a couple of reasons: #1. He was the good ole Rev. Shadrack and #2. Shadrack never turned down Peaches request for some head; Shadrack was always willing to please!

Shadrack locked up the church, got in his car, and headed for Brooklyn. He was smiling from ear to ear; first Peaches, then Anthony.

****

While Shadrack and Anthony were on their separate missions, Sylvia was on the New Jersey Turnpike, headed to the nation's capital. All she could think about was the confrontation she had with Anthony. In his fifteen years of existence, she had never raised a hand to him like she did today! But he had crossed the line! How could he stand there and spew lies like that, about the man who clothed and fed him for the last ten years of his life? It had to be a demon, Sylvia thought; that was the only logical explanation. Then a thought ran across her mind… could Anthony actually be telling the truth? Sylvia quickly dismissed the thought. Sure, Shadrack hadn't made love to her in over a year, but she knew it was the pressures of being a pastor. She quickly tossed all thoughts of this nonsense out the window. One thing was for sure. And that was Shadrack took damn good care of her! She quickly determined she wasn't going to lose her Gucci, Prada, Burberry, Chanel and Dolce for anyone. Not to mention a new Benz every two years!

Chapter 7

Ant and Preme had been sitting in the same position, close to the cell bars for well over four hours. Preme had listened to Ant recant the horrid details of his life. Ant took his time, and often had to stop to get his emotions under control. Preme didn't say much, he mostly listened, and occasionally he'd say "damn", or "that sick ass bastard" (of course he was referring to Shadrack). And when Ant told him what his mom decided, Preme called her a "dumb ass bitch".

"Ant, it's nearly 5 am, and we've been sitting here for over four hours. I know this hasn't been easy, retelling all this mess. But in the long run, you'll be glad you did. My suggestion, is that we get some sleep, and if you want… we can do this again tonight. Honestly, I don't know what to say, other than I'm sorry you had to go through all that bullshit. I do know, that had I known you back then, you wouldn't have gone through that shit; I would've killed his fat ass. But rest assured, you'll never have to go through it again. That I promise." Preme didn't know what else to say, nor did he know how to fully express his need to help Ant by any means necessary.

Ant sat there somewhat amazed that he shared his life with someone he met less than a week ago. For some strange unknown reason, he trusted Preme… and that worried him above anything else. At this point in his life, he didn't think he could live through another betrayal. "Thanks. Yea, we can finish talking later. I've told you all that, so I might as well tell you the whole thing" said Ant.

"Get some rest Ant. Thanks for trusting me. I know it wasn't easy. Talk to you later." With nothing to be said, they both fell back onto their beds, but neither one slept.

****

Usually on Sunday's, after Ant has fed the keep-locks, he would attend the service in the chapel. He would sit in the back and listen to the songs and the message. The Chaplain at this facility wasn't the greatest of preachers, but he wasn't the worst. He kept his message simple, and didn't try to be someone he wasn't. Ant respected him for that. Despite all the hell Ant went through, he still loved the Lord, and he didn't blame him for Shadrack's actions. He was grateful to God, that he wasn't messed up in the head like so many others who had been through the very same thing as he did. He had read stories from people who went through similar situations, and were on drugs, suicidal, and repeated the same cycle by doing the same horrible acts to others. Sure, Ant had a problem with his extreme lust for pussy, which at times made him jerk off… sometimes up to three times a day. Now, he hardly ever jerks off, and when he does, he would fall into such a deep conviction, mostly because he remembered one of the lines from Mother Green's letter, "be everything Shadrack is not". And to accomplish that, Anthony had to get his act together.

Ant figured he'd skip service today, and catch a nap after returning from his duties. When he got to his cell, he noticed Preme standing at his gate, dressed in a fresh pair of state issued green pants, a new white tee and a pair of the new $250.00 Jordan's. "Hurry up, they'll be calling services in about ten minutes." Ant had not seen Preme in a service before, so he figured he would be easy to discourage. "I ain't going to service this morning. I'm gonna lay back and chill."

"What you mean you ain't going? After all God has brought you through, how can you not give thanks every chance you get? And, I haven't been to church in I don't know how long… it's your responsibility, as a believer to encourage me to go and even go with me!" Preme did have a point. Plus, if he laid up in the cell, all he would do is think on all the mess from his past. Ant rushed into his cell and quickly changed. He too put on a brand-new state issued pair of pants, one of the sweat shirts Preme had sent him, and a pair of new Timbs. When the Protestant service (Ant had no idea what that was. Growing up, all he knew was Baptist, AME, AME Zion, Pentecostal, Apostolic, Church of God and COGIC… but never Protestant) was called, Ant came out of his cell and stood there, waiting for Preme's cell to open. When it finally opened, Preme came out and they both proceeded through the gallery and to the line forming downstairs.

Once they were in the chapel (which is also the auditorium), Ant and Preme sat down side by side, in the last row. The Chaplain got up, asked everyone to stand and proceeded to pray the opening prayer. Once the prayer was over, he told everyone they could be seated, and began to address the congregation.

"God bless you all my brothers. The Lord placed it on my heart to do something a little different today. I'm not going to preach, but rather I'm going to open up the service for testimonies and song. Now, let me say this, this is not an opportunity for you to preach. A testimony, is what God is doing in your life. Let's also be mindful that other brothers may want to share as well, so let's keep it as brief as possible. If there is a song on your heart, feel free to share it. Amen. Now, who will be first?"

Two brothers immediately raised their hands. The first got up and told how God delivered him from cigarettes and how much he loved the Lord. The second got up and attempted to sing "No Weapon Formed Against Me". The rendition was so horrid, that if Fred Hammond would've heard it, it would've made him not want to eat for 40 days and 40 nights! However, the brother was giving God the glory. While he was giving everyone in attendance massive ear trauma, I mean, he was sliding ALL OVER the musical scale...Ant felt Preme nudge him. "Yo, why don't you go next and sing a little sum'n, sum'n? We could certainly use it after this cat just murdered a perfectly good song. Whoever that song belongs to, needs to prosecute him to the fullest extent of the law, making sure he gets life without the possiblity of parole!"

Preme was visibly disgusted with the brother's efforts. "So, are you going to sing or what? Preme inquired a second time. "No, I'm gonna pass. And keep it down, we're still in church."

"Come on! Sing a song and stop playing ghetto games." Just then, the brother finished the song and took his seat. No one moved and just expected the next man to get up. All of a sudden Preme jumped up, cleared his throat and began speaking. "Good morning church. I don't have a testimony... however, I do have a request, if that's okay with you Chaplain?"

"Why sure brother, help yourself."

"Thank you, Chaplain. This is my first time here in service and my best friend, Bro. Ant Morgan brought me here today." Anthony was so embarrassed, that he wished the floor underneath him would open up and just swallow him. "Bro. Anthony is a great singer and spent his life, prior to his incarceration, singing in churches all over the New York City area. It would really mean a great deal to me, and it would keep me coming to service faithfully. Well, except on the Sunday's that I have my visits, if he would sing us a song this morning." Preme stood there looking down at Ant, and then began clapping, as did the rest of the congregation.

"Come on Bro. Ant, let the Lord use you this morning. Plus we want to make sure this brother here continues to come to service. Amen." Said the Chaplain, who in turn got an Amen from the congregation as well. Then more of the congregants began standing, turning towards Ant and began clapping. Ant finally stood up, looked at Preme, rolled his eyes, and finally made his way to the front of the church. Ant hadn't sung in a minute, and didn't really know what to sing. There were three musicians in attendance that morning. A brother on a Yamaha DX-7 keyboard, one on the drums, and one on the bass guitar. All three were good musicians. It was said that they were cousins and grew up playing at their grandfather's church (Church of God in Christ), on Adelphi Street in Brooklyn. It was also said that one night two years ago, the cousins had backslid and went out drinking. All three were pissy drunk, when the oldest (the one on the keyboard) got behind the wheel of his father's Lincoln Town car, while the other two rode shot gun (all three of them squeezed up in the front) and went for a joy ride. Apparently, they hit a twenty-year-old female college student on Myrtle and Classon Ave, and fled the scene. A bystander happened to witness the whole thing, called the police, and in a little over an hour and a half, all three were in jail. Luckily, the girl survived, so they're only serving a five-year sentence.

Ant took the microphone once he got up front. He took a deep breath and began talking. "God bless you all. I wasn't prepared to sing today, but a very special lady once told me, that only what you do for Christ will last. I need y'all's prayers this morning." Anthony bowed his head, closed his eyes like he was praying, and held the mic tightly with both hands. A second later, he opened his eyes, turned his head to the brother on the keyboard and told him to put him in the key of "E flat". The brother on the keys quickly switched the key he was softly playing, to accommodate Ant. Finally, he opened his mouth and began singing. Ant chose an old hymn "Amazing Grace Shall Always Be", and just made it his own. At first, no one made a sound, they were just captivated by his soaring vocals. Even the musicians were blown away and had to really concentrate on their playing so they wouldn't mess up.

Ant felt a peace come over him, similar to that night he sang "Faith That Conquers" at his old church, and Mother Green had prayed for him. He began to hit notes and do riffs that he didn't know he had in him; this was his gift. Man, by the time he started singing the chorus, people were standing on their feet urging him on. The Chaplain was standing with his eyes closed and his arms raised. Some got down on their knees in worship. Preme stood there with his eyes full of tears, unable to move. Ant had told him he could sing, but he was not expecting this. R. Kelly, Sisco, Boys II Men, Jodeci, RL nor Tevin Campbell had anything on Ant. Preme knew right then and there, that he would sacrifice everything to help Ant.

When Ant hit that final note, it was one that would've made Patti LaBelle, the queen of notes, crown Ant the king! The church was in an uproar, to the point that two officers came rushing in, to make sure a riot had not started! The musicians being from the Church of God in Christ, knew just what to do. As if planned, they began playing a fast-rhythmic beat. Once the beat got going, some began jumping, while others clapped, and some even got in the aisles and danced as if they were in their local neighborhood Pentecostal church. Ant simply replaced the mic into its stand and made his way back to his seat next to Preme. When he reached his seat, Preme looked at Ant like he was seeing him for the first time. Ant too stood there looking at Preme, and at that very moment, Ant knew he could trust Preme with his life if need be. Then as if on cue, they embraced.

****

That night, after final count had been taken and the gallery was quiet, Preme and Ant took the same positions as the night before, by the gate, with the mirror in Preme's hand. "Man! I wasn't expecting you to blow like that. The only other time a singer moved me like you did was when I saw Patti LaBelle at the Apollo; I was crying like a bitch."

"Thanks. And Patti is the truth. Can't nobody sing like her. And I mean **NOBODY. T**hat includes Aretha." Ant stressed that nobody, for he didn't feel worthy to even be mentioned in the same sentence with a legend like Patti.

"You ever thought about recording? Actually singing for a living?"

"Yea… but you gotta know somebody."

"You know somebody… me! And I'm gonna see to it that your dream comes true. Trust that." Ant was touched and didn't know what to say. A few seconds later he found his voice. "Well, I guess I might as well pick up where I left off last night."

Chapter 8

When Anthony reached South Road it was completely dark, except for the moon and stars that lit the strip. Years ago, the bulbs in the street had been knocked out, and the city didn't see any sense in replacing them. Ant knew all he had to do was walk, show no sign of fear, and someone would emerge out of nowhere and inquire about his needs. Sure enough, he hadn't even walked an entire block when someone appeared from an alley and asked Anthony what he wanted.

"What you need son, rock?" This question came from a seedy looking character, who couldn't have been more than twenty-years-old. He had gold on all his teeth and his complexion was what old folks used to call "blue-black". And had it not been for his gold teeth and eyes, he would be invisible in the night.

"Naw I need some heat" Anthony replied, hoping he had used the proper slang term for "gun". Midnight, that's what the streets called him, stepped closer to Anthony and really looked at him. "Hey, aren't you that preacher's kid? The choir boy? Yeah, you sung at my cousin's funeral last year! Yo, you can sing your ass off; I bet that gets you plenty of pussy! And those light ass eyes probably help you too. Yeah, you can blow, my aunt said that whenever she gets sad about Ronnie, my cousin who got killed… she thinks of that song you sung. What you doing all the way over here? This ain't no place for a good Christian boy like yourself."

Anthony thought this mofo would never shut up, and was appalled that this cat even knew who he was. He had to stay focused. Anthony knew he couldn't worry about all that. He needed protection and he wasn't leaving until he got it. "I told you, I need some heat."

"What the fuck you need heat for? You got beef with a cat? Tell me who and where, and me and my boys will go handle it. That's the least I can do. Besides, you wouldn't even take any money for singing at Ronnie's funeral." Midnight then placed his thumb and middle finger in his mouth and let forth a whistle like siren. Two huge dark figures appeared from out of nowhere and stopped where Ant and Midnight were standing.

"Yo, you remember that kid that sang at Ronnie's funeral, the choir boy? The one that had everybody open?" Neither of the two spoke, but rather shook their heads in recognition that they remembered. "He's got some beef and came looking for some heat. I told him we'll take care of it for him." Midnight explained. Again, the two Biggie Smalls look-a-likes nodded their heads in agreement. Ant was starting to get really pissed. He didn't need this shit right now… and it showed when he spoke.

"Look, I don't have beef. I just need some protection you heard?" He was trying hard to imitate the hood vernacular that he often heard used in school.

"Who the hell you need protection from? Someone at the church?" Anthony determined right then and there, that Midnight was an asshole! He sounded more like the fucking District Attorney, asking all these damn questions, than the two-bit hustler he claimed to be.

"You know what, if you don't wanna sell me no heat, I'll take my cheddar elsewhere." Anthony stated and stood there waiting for a response. And the one he got, just made him even more angry. "Cheddar? Did he say Cheddar?" Midnight turned and asked fake Biggie #1 and

#2, who just nodded. "Yo, we haven't heard cheddar in about twenty years!" Anthony was livid. Here he was, trying to take care of business, and this spook was making fun of him.

"I'll go further down; good lookin." Ant said and began walking down the road, but Midnight called him back. "Yo choir boy, what kinda heat you want?" Anthony stopped, turned around and walked back over to Midnight and his boys.

"I need a gun." Anthony stated, wondering if this dude was retarded.

"I know that, but what kind? A Mack, Glock, 357? Tell me what you want."

"Something small and light weight… something that will fit in my pocket."

"I got just the thing." Midnight bent over, lifted up one of his pants legs and retrieved a small silver handgun from his ankle holster. "This here my man is a .25. It holds up to six shots. It's not that good from far away, but close up, it packs some punch!" Anthony took the gun from Midnight and passed it from one hand to the other. It was light and could easily be concealed right in the hole of his mattress.

"How much you want for it?"

"Well, normally I'd let it go for no less than $300." Anthony reached in his pocket and pulled out the knot he had removed from his mattress and began counting.

"Hold up, choir boy. I said normally. I didn't say I was charging you $300. You did my family a good deed, so now it's my turn. Give me $50 and she's yours. Anthony didn't say anything. He searched for a 50-dollar bill, and when he found it, gave it to Midnight. "Be careful with that shorty, it's loaded. If you need anything else, I'm here every night." Anthony gave Midnight a pound and thought about giving the two Biggie's one, but thought better of it. "Yo, keep singing too. My mom's and aunt would've kicked my ass if I had taken the whole $300 from you." Anthony shook his head in disbelief and got the hell outta there.

****

Anthony got back, finding the house still empty. Shadrack must still be at the church. It was just after 9pm and he needed to contemplate his next move. He remembered the booty call he had scheduled for tonight. He quickly called, telling her something important came up and he would call her tomorrow. So, what now? Anthony had no friends and nowhere he could hide out at. He had about six hundred dollars, but that wouldn't take him very far. Mother Green came to Anthony's mind, but she was gone now. In an instant, another person came to mind. Someone he hadn't seen or spoken to in three years; Harold. Anthony raced into his room, opened his sock drawer and began searching until he found what he was looking for. Anthony held the business card Harold had given him after Mother Green's funeral. Anthony thought about all the things Harold had stated that day, about everybody not being like him (Shadrack), and to call him when he was ready. Anthony sat on the bed and just stared at the card, as hundreds of thoughts ran through his mind. Did Harold really mean those things? Could he be trusted, or was he just another Shadrack without the backwards collar?

Anthony quickly fell into conviction over the last thought. Mother Green had gone out of her way to express her love and concern of him to Harold, and he was just following in his mother's footsteps. Or was he? "Why hadn't he called?" Anthony thought. Then he realized something… he could sit there, and go back and forth with questions that he had no answers to. Or he could pick up the phone and call Harold. And with that, Anthony picked up the phone that was resting next to his bed, and dialed Harold's home number. After three rings, an adolescent female answered.

"Hello"

"May I speak to Harold please?"

"One second". Anthony heard the phone being placed on a hard surface and heard the girl yell.

"Daddy, someone's on the phone for you"

"Alright sweetheart, I'm coming" Anthony heard Harold say.

"Hello" Harold said upon picking up the phone.

"Harold?" Anthony asked, sounding more like an eight-year-old than fifteen.

"This is he. Who is this?"

"It's Anthony. Anthony Morgan. I was the one…"

"I remember who you are. I was starting to wonder if I'd ever hear from you. I've often thought of you and wondered how you were doing."

"I wish I could say that I was alright."

"Talk to me Anthony… what's going on?"

"Do you still have my letter? The one Mother Green wrote me?"

"Of course I have it. I told you I would keep it for you." Anthony just sat there holding the phone, and Harold just waited. Finally, it was Harold who broke the silence.

"Anthony, what's going on? What has Shadrack done?" Anthony didn't respond, but Harold knew he was still on the line. When Harold spoke again, his voice had raised a notch, due to fear of what Anthony was not saying.

"Anthony, please talk to me. Do you need me to come there?"

"I'll call you back later... for my letter."

"Anthony, please don't hang up on me. You called me, so you must need me. I am here for you if you allow me to be."

"I'll call you back soon Harold." Harold was crazed with anxiety and concern.

"Anthony, just sit still. I'm on my way. I'll be there in a few hours." Anthony quietly replaced the phone back in its cradle.

When Anthony hung up the phone with Harold, he sat in the dark for an undetermined amount of time. The phone had rung several times, but Anthony sat there as if he didn't even hear it. Looking at his watch, he realized it was after 11pm. Fatigue had plagued him, and he needed to rest. He kicked his sneakers off, removed his newly purchased weapon from his pocket and placed it under his pillow. He laid down and hoped he wouldn't have to use it tonight.

****

Shadrack was driving on the Brooklyn/Queens Expressway, approaching the Van Wyck Expressway. He was returning from an always adventurous time with Peaches, the homosexual booster, that he bought all their clothes from. He now had a trunk full of designer suits, shirts, ties, purses, shoes of all makes, and even various body scents. As he drove, he thought about Peaches' antics tonight. Normally, Peaches only charge him 35% of what the items were priced, but when he bought in bulk, as he did tonight… Peaches would only charge him 25% of the total price for all the items. Tonight, Peaches wanted to play games and add some adventure to their already special relationship. Peaches had told Shadrack that he not only had to give him the entire 35% for the bulk, he also added an additional 5% as well. Shadrack couldn't believe his sanctified ears. Peaches gave some lame excuse about something coming up, and that was the reason he needed the extra money. Shadrack knew Peaches wanted some head, but was just too reserved to ask for it.

"What do I have to do to get my usual 25%... give you some head maybe?" Shadrack smiled and awaited Peaches response… he was sure that's all he wanted.

"I'm saying, you can do that if you want, but I still need the money. I have something that I must take care of Shadrack."

"Peaches, what do you have to take care of, that would take every dime that I have in my pocket?"

"No disrespect Rev., but my business is my fuckin' business. I don't ask you the details of what goes on in the Brown house-hold, nor do I ask what's going on at Another Greater Chance or whatever the fuck your church's name is. I would appreciate it if you would afford me the same respect. Thank you." Shadrack knew that was a bunch of bullshit; Peaches wanted something, but instead of just asking, he wanted to play games.

"I'm just trying to help you brother Maurice."

"It's P-E-A-C-H-E-S... Peaches, you fat fuck!"

"Yes, Peaches. I was just trying to show some concern, and for the record; my church's name is The Greater Second Chance Love Revival Tabernacle."

"Whatever"

"Now Peaches, are you in a rush to go anywhere?" Peaches knew he had him. He knew that Shadrack's fat ass would do anything to save a buck, or maybe that's just what he wanted people to think, and was really just willing to do whatever. "Why?"

"I was thinking that maybe we could find a little out of the way motel, check in, have a few drinks and see what happens. It would certainly be better than sitting here in the car, under this damn bridge." They had been sitting in Shadrack's car, in a deserted area under the Brooklyn Bridge. "Mm... First off, I didn't know Reverends drank?"

"Well, normally I don't touch spirits, but tonight I'm willing to make an exception... being that I'm with such fine company tonight." This asshole was really aiming to please tonight, thought Peaches. He was curious to see how far the good ole Rev would go. "Secondly, you want to go to a motel, just to give me some head? I told you before, I am not a child! You will never stick ya little member in me, nor will I give you head."

"Peaches, I never suggested any of those things; I remember your conditions, and I'd never try to override them. Never!" This dude was the biggest bullshitter on earth, both in the pulpit and in his regular day to day life. But one day, his shit was gonna catch up to him.

"Imma let you know off bat, I've got my blade on me… if you try and pull something, I will slice and dice ya ass." Peaches warned Shadrack. "Believe that!"

Chapter 9

Forty-five minutes later, they pulled into the parking lot of some shady looking motel, somewhere off of Queens Blvd. They would have made it there sooner, but they had to find a liquor store that wouldn't ask Peaches for I.D., because Shadrack was afraid if he went into any liquor store, someone would recognize him. The third store they found didn't ask for I.D., Peaches told Shadrack, after returning with the bag of goods. He was sure the owner of the store (an old white dude), wanted to swing an episode... which Peaches politely turned down.

Shadrack sent Peaches into the office to secure the room, while he waited in the car. He told Peaches to secure the room for 4 hours, which would cost about $40. Shadrack couldn't wait for Peaches to hurry up! If there was ever a time he needed to "let his hair down", it was tonight. Peaches came out of the office, key in hand, and walked towards the various rooms until he reached 106 and entered. Shadrack waited about a minute, looked around to make sure the coast was clear, exited the car and made a quick dash to the room.

Shadrack entered the room and closed the door behind him, as Peaches took one of the bottles from the bag, quickly opened it, took a long swig and flopped down on the lumpy bed. Peaches figured he'd let Shadrack initiate tonight's festivities. Shadrack took one of the bottles from the bag and sat next to Peaches on the bed. He grabbed Peaches knee and said: "So, what do you suggest we do tonight my dearest Peaches?"

"This was your fuckin idea Rev.! You mean to tell me you had nothing in mind when you suggested we come here?" Peaches replied, realizing he was tired of playing this damn game with Shadrack. "Shadrack… take ya damn clothes off and get down on your hands and knees." Peaches demanded.

"Good God almighty; I thought you'd never ask!" Four hours later, Shadrack was on his way home with a trunk full of clothes (which he only paid 25%), a still pulsating rectum and a huge smile on his face. Shadrack steered the car off the Van Wyck and in the direction of home.

****

Anthony was awakened by the sound of the front door being opened and then shut. He looked at the clock on his night stand and saw that it was just after midnight. He laid there like he was still asleep, listening to the various movements Shadrack made throughout the house. Anthony caressed the gun resting under his pillow, praying he wouldn't have to use it. He laid there for over an hour, listening to Shadrack's movements. It seemed to Anthony that Shadrack was occupied with whatever he was doing and would not be stopping by for a visit. It was around 1:30 am when Anthony dozed off to sleep.

The clock on the night stand read 3:15 am, and Anthony was asleep on his stomach with his hands under his pillow, his right hand holding the gun, when he heard his bedroom door open as Shadrack entered. The door closed and there was no movement for several minutes. Anthony suspected that Shadrack was standing there watching him, trying to see if he was really asleep. He thought the hard pumping of his heart was a sure giveaway. Anthony couldn't see Shadrack because the way he was laying, his back facing the door. However, it didn't take long before Shadrack made his presence known. He ran his hands across Anthony's still clothed backside, which caused Anthony to stir involuntarily. Shadrack continued to run his hand up and down Anthony's back. "Come on and wake up. I haven't bothered you in some time now. It's just you and me here, and we don't get chances like this too often. The good Lord wants us to take advantage of them."

Anthony slowly opened his eyes to find Shadrack standing at the side of his bed, butt naked and still caressing his back. Anthony had the gun in his hand, still under the pillow. Still hoping this fool would leave and he wouldn't have to cap his fat ass. Shadrack had stopped caressing his back, and was now trying to pull his pants down. "I'm gonna tell you this ONE TIME, Shadrack. Walk out of this room now and leave me alone! You walk out now and I'll forget this incident, as well as the others. You don't walk out of here... I promise your fat ass will regret it!"

"Nigga! Who the hell you think you talking to? This is my damn house! I pay all the bills and I take care of your loose ass. That two-cent job you have doesn't take care of shit up in this bitch! You need to show a bit more respect boy, for the scripture says *"honor your father and mother".* Now pull your pants down and give me what I need!" Anthony continued to lay on his stomach. All the while Shadrack was talking, Anthony had his eyes closed and when he spoke, he continued to keep them closed.

"I told you... I was only gonna tell you once! I haven't changed my mind. This is your final warning!" Shadrack had been standing there with both hands on his hips, waiting for Anthony to follow his instructions. When Anthony didn't and gave the "final warning", Shadrack became furious and began yelling and pulling on Anthony's pants. "You threatening me in my house? Now I'm gonna fuck you with no grease, you pretty eyed bitch!" Anthony removed his hand from under the pillow and rolled over. He pointed the gun directly at Shadrack and said: "Back the fuck up!"

Shadrack was caught completely off guard by the sight of the gun. The excitement that Shadrack once showed, dwindled down to almost non-existent. It was several minutes before anyone moved or said anything. Shadrack gained his composure and spoke: You think that little ass toy gun scares me? You think that's gonna stop me from getting what's rightfully mines? Shadrack stood there and began to stroke himself until he was erect. When that was accomplished, he began inching towards the bed again.

Anthony had both hands on the gun, which was still pointed at Shadrack. "You might as well turn over… cause you're gonna get fucked tonight."

Shadrack was turned on more by Anthony's performance than anything else; first Peaches and now Anthony. He couldn't wait any longer… Shadrack was right up on the gun Anthony held. He went to move Anthony's hand and in an instant, there was a bright flash in the room and an explosion like sound. Anthony's arms buckled slightly and he fell back on the bed, with his eyes still glued on Shadrack. Shadrack stood there, eye bulging and a sharp pain in his stomach. He moved his hand to his stomach and at the same time, his knees buckled and he fell to the floor. Shadrack could feel the hot, sticky liquid sliding down his stomach. He removed his hand, moved it to his face and just stared. Twenty seconds later, Shadrack was face down on the floor. The only sounds that could be heard was Shadrack's labored breathing, and a barely audible moan.

Anthony got up from the bed, gun still in hand as he stood over Shadrack, looking down at his limp form. Rage and fury from eight years of torment engulfed him, as he began kicking Shadrack in the ribs. "I hate you, you fucking pervert. I told you to leave but you wouldn't. Take this you sick bastard." Anthony continued to kick Shadrack with all his might. As he continued to kick him, his voice began to crack and tears fell from his eyes. Finally, Anthony fell to his knees, almost identical to the way Shadrack fell. He let the gun fall from his hand, covered his face and began to sob in anguish.

"Oh my God! What have you done?" The voice came from the entrance of Anthony's bedroom, behind him. The voice startled him and immediately his sobbing stopped. He turned around at the same time that Sylvia began yelling & screaming. "I knew when I left that the devil had you, and that's why I came back. Look at what you've done!" Sylvia ran into the room, pushed past Anthony and kneeled down by Shadrack's side. She struggled to turn him over. For reason's Anthony couldn't explain, he moved to assist Sylvia in turning Shadrack over. "Don't you dare touch him. Get thee back Satan! You did this!"

Anthony froze in his tracks and stared blankly at Sylvia. He couldn't believe she had called him Satan and blamed him. "No! Satan is on the floor, and if anyone did this… it was you!" Anthony yelled. Sylvia got up from the floor and went to the telephone. She dialed 911 while Anthony was still yelling. "You married him! You were too blind to see the shit he was doing to me, or did you just look the other way for jewelry and clothes? No… YOU DID THIS!"

"Yes, my husband has been shot and he needs an ambulance right away." Sylvia proceeded to give the 911 operator the address and informed them that Shadrack was still breathing. Before she hung up the phone, she looked over at Anthony and spoke again into the phone. "I also need the police; the shooter is still in the house."

Sylvia hung up the phone and went back by Shadrack's side. Anthony stood there looking at the two of them with pure disgust, then went to the living room until the ambulance and the police arrived.

****

Twenty minutes later, an unconscious Shadrack was being rushed into the ambulance, while a handcuffed Anthony was being placed into a squad car. After Shadrack was placed in the ambulance, Sylvia jumped in and sat by his side, holding his hand. When the paramedics first arrived, they quickly went to work on Shadrack. The police had arrived not long after. The paramedics had informed the officers that Shadrack had lost a great deal of blood, but the wound doesn't seem life threatening; he's expected to make a full recovery.

Once Sylvia knew Shadrack would be okay, she turned her attention to the police. She told them about the huge fight she had with Anthony prior to leaving for D.C. However, she left out all the things he had accused Shadrack of. Sylvia told the officers how out of the blue, Anthony began to change. How he began showing nothing but contempt for Shadrack, despite how much Shadrack loved and cared for him   since he was five-years-old. She continued the tale, stating that she felt the need to come back because she believed Anthony was demon possessed and could not be trusted. She went on to tell how upon entering the house, she heard the gun shot and raced in knowing Anthony had done something horrible. She told them that she found Shadrack on the floor of Anthony's bedroom, bleeding and being kicked and yelled at by Anthony.

Now, previous to the police and the paramedics coming, and while Anthony was sitting in the living room, Sylvia had retrieved Shadrack's bathrobe from the bedroom and somehow managed to get it on him. What Sylvia didn't realize is that the paramedics would notice that there was no bullet hole in the robe. Therefore they'd know that he was originally naked when he was shot. Fortunately, the paramedics shared this piece of info with the officers, and they held off asking Sylvia about it until they questioned Anthony. They had their suspicions already... but they waited before passing judgement.

As Anthony sat in the back of the squad car, after admitting to the officers that he did indeed shoot Shadrack, he looked out at the crowd of spectators and the press. He couldn't believe it had really come to this. From the moment he was brought out of the house, cameras had been snapping non-stop. Even as he sat in the squad car. But Anthony didn't care about what they did or said.   All he knew was... he'd never be a victim again.

Chapter 10

Anthony sat alone in the interrogation room at the 103 Precinct. It was early Saturday morning and he had been sitting in the room for about an hour. He knew they would be coming in any moment wanting answers. The question in his mind was; would they believe him? No sooner that question came to his mind, the door had opened and in walked two detectives. One Caucasian male in his mid-30's and the other was an African American male, about 50-years-old. "Alright Anthony, I'm detective Malone" said the black guy "and this is Detective Reilly. Why don't you tell us what brought this on?"

Three hours later, after telling the detectives his story eight times, and answering hundreds of questions, Anthony found himself sitting in a small cell, all alone. He wasn't sorry at all for what he did to Shadrack. Shadrack caused him more hurt & pain than he could ever fully express. The only thing that really scared Anthony at this point, was going to prison! There was no doubt in his mind that he was going. The question was; could he survive? He had heard too many stories, read too many books, and saw way too many television shows as to what goes on in prison. There were people just like Shadrack, even in the adolescent facilities. So many questions ran through his mind, and all the logical answers scared the hell out of him.

"You made the morning papers Morgan." Anthony looked up to see a uniformed cop standing in front of the cell. "Take a look for yourself." The officer placed the paper on the cell bars and walked off. Anthony got up, took the paper and sat down. He opened the paper and **WAS NOT** ready for what he saw. On the front of the Daily News was a picture of Anthony handcuffed and being led out of the house by two officers. But it was the headline that shook his very foundation.

"Choir Boy Shoots Pastor/Step Dad"

Anthony was well aware of what he did, but seeing the picture and the headlines… that took things to an entirely different level for him emotionally. No one would ever see what Shadrack had done, but they would always see Anthony as the "troubled teen" that shot his mother's husband. Anthony realized he could not change what people thought, nor should he really care. He was the one that endured Shadrack's violations for eight long years. Anyone who could not see or understand his plight, FUCK 'EM!

Anthony decided to read the article and see just how troubled they portrayed him. This is what it said:

Early this morning, on the quiet Jamaica Estates block, the Rev. Shadrack E. Brown, pastor of The Greater Second Chance Love Revival Tabernacle, also located in Jamaica, Queens, was shot by his fifteen-year-old step-son, Anthony Morgan. Rev. Brown was shot in the stomach around 3:30 am. It is unclear as to the cause of the shooting, but what is clear is that upon their arrival, the paramedics found the Rev. wounded on the floor of his step-son's bedroom. It also appears that Rev. Brown was completely naked at the time of the shooting.

Anthony Morgan is a sophomore at Bayside High School, and maintained an "A" average. Anthony has made a name for himself throughout the Tri-State area as a renowned vocalist and musician, signing at numerous church functions. Anthony is also employed at the Western Beef on Merrick Blvd., and is the youngest part-time manager in the store's history. The Rev. Brown is expected to make a full recovery and Anthony will be charged with attempted murder.

Anthony put the paper down, sat back and just closed his eyes.

Two days later, after being arraigned and placed in the Queens House of Detention (QHD) Facility, Anthony was on his way to the visiting room. He had no idea who could be there to see him. Surely it wasn't Sylvia. Sylvia had been standing in the packed court room when Anthony was arraigned. When he was being brought out, their eyes met… and if looks could kill, Anthony would've been dead on-site. The look Sylvia gave him was one of pure hatred, disgust and contempt. Sylvia then turned and walked out of the court room… so Anthony knew she wasn't in the visiting room waiting to see him.

Anthony reached the visiting room and was directed to sit at the small table, with a single chair on each side of the table. He was informed by the CO that his visitor would be in shortly. Anthony looked around the room and saw several inmates enjoying their hour visit, along with others just like him, awaiting the entrance of their visitors. This was an entirely new world for Anthony. Since being brought to QHD, he hadn't been out of his cell until today. He hadn't eaten anything, nor had he spoken to any of the other inmates on the tier. Several of them came to his cell and tried to converse with him, but Anthony trusted no one. Anthony had taken his first shower since being arrested, only after being informed that he had a visit… and that shower lasted a hot sixty seconds.

After what seemed like forever, at the front of the visiting room was a huge sliding door. It began to open. Once fully opened, a throng of people entered, all looking over the visiting room, hoping to quickly spot their loved ones. There were mostly women, some with children, and a couple of men. The last one to enter was someone Anthony recognized and knew was his visitor; it was Harold.

Harold stood just inside the visiting room door, looking for Anthony. By this time, just about everyone who had entered found who they were looking for, so it didn't take Harold long to spot Anthony. When Harold located him, he made his way through the masses of people and tables, to where Anthony was seated. When Harold finally reached the table, he stood there expecting Anthony to greet him with a hug. Harold could only imagine the pain and the grief Anthony must be going through. He knew the kid needed love, but he would not force him. Once Harold realized that Anthony was not going to get up, he took a seat on the other side of the table, facing Anthony. Harold sat there and studied Anthony, who sat there with his head hung low. "Anthony, how are you?" Anthony continued to sit there with his head hung. So many things ran through his mind. Could he trust Harold, or was he just like everyone else? His own mother turned her back on him, so could he really expect anyone else to be there for him? Then he remembered that Harold was Mother Green's son, and he began to feel the doubt slip away. Before Anthony could open his mouth to answer Harold's question, Harold spoke again.

"Anthony, listen to me. My mother loved you as if you were her own. To her, you were her son and that makes you my brother. I flew all the way over here because I knew you needed someone. My wife Denise would have come as well, if we had someone to watch the kids on such short notice. We love you and we're willing to do what we can for you. Now, will you tell me how you are and what happened?"

Anthony finally lifted his head and spoke. "I'm alright for someone who just tried to kill his mother's husband."

"Where did you get the gun Anthony?"

"Don't call me that anymore" Harold was caught completely off guard by that one. "Anthony is your name, right?"

"It **WAS** my name. Anthony was an innocent young kid. I am not innocent anymore, nor am I a kid." Harold's heart went out to the boy, but he could understand what Anthony was saying.

"What should I call you?"

"Just call me Ant."

"Okay Ant. So, tell me what happened?"

"I shot the sick bastard and that's the end of it." Harold didn't expect Ant to be this withdrawn. The years between the last time Harold had seen Ant to now had not been kind to him.

"What was going on that made you shoot him Ant? I have my ideas, but if I'm going to help you, I need to be sure."

"If you have an idea, then you already know" replied Ant.

"How long was he abusing you?" Harold asked, trying hard to hold back his rage. He wished he could get his hands on Shadrack's pedophile ass. Harold was sure he could kill him with his bare hands.

"Since I was seven; eight years old."

"What about Sylvia?"

"What about her? Maybe she knew, but was too caught up in being the first lady, with all the clothes, jewelry and cars… I guess she looked the other way. Friday, before she left, I told her everything and she slapped me. She told me I was demon possessed." Harold was beyond furious now, and he knew he bests not run into Shadrack or Sylvia, or he'd be in jail too.

"Alright, they've charged you with attempted murder and a weapons charge. Do you have an attorney?"

"Yeah, some whacko appointed by the state, who told me he'd try to get me twenty years flat. He wasn't even concerned, nor did he ask why I did what I did." Anthony finished speaking, took a deep breath, and released it. He felt like the weight of the world was resting on his shoulders.

"When I leave here, I have an appointment with a criminal lawyer who's supposed to be one of the best; he seems to be interested in your case. We'll fire the whacko and get someone who's gonna work for you. I'll have to leave in a day or two, but not before I hire someone, go collect your things from Shadrack's, and go shopping for the things you'll need in here. On my way out, I'll check and see what you can and can't have okay?"

Ant nodded a yes and Harold continued. "I'm gonna have to go soon, so I won't be late for the meeting with the lawyer. But I'll be back to see you and bring you somethings before I fly back home. I want you to know, you will get through this. We are family. I want you to call the house tonight. Denise wants to get to know you and hear for herself, that you're okay. Got it?"

"Yeah, I got it."

"Alright man, let me run. BE safe in here. The lawyer will be here tomorrow, provided he takes the case, which I'm almost positive he will! And I'll be back the day after tomorrow." Harold got up from the table and put out his hand for Ant to shake it; he really wanted to give him a hug, but he knew not to rush him. Ant shook his hand and Harold turned and headed towards the exit.

"Harold" Ant called. Harold stopped, turned and waited. "Thank you." Harold nodded and proceeded through the exit. Anthony sat there, and for the first time since the shooting, said a silent prayer of thanks. He thanked God for his life, for Harold & Denise, and for being free! He might be locked up... but he was forever free.

****

The faint glimpse of sunrise could be seen in the distance. Ant and Preme had been in the very same position they were in the night before, close by the gate, with Preme holding the mirror for hours. Preme sat there stunned by the events of Ant's life. After listening to Ant the night before, Preme didn't think he could become angrier, but after last night's talk... Preme was beyond angry; he was livid. His heart went out to Ant, but he knew he would be okay... because he vowed to make sure of that.

After all of that, Preme didn't know what to say to break the walls of silence. But he knew he had to say something. "You alright?" Ant took a deep breath and nodded.

"Yeah, why wouldn't I be, after all of this? And in about three months, I'll be returning to society after doing ten years for shooting my mother's husband, who started fucking me at the age of seven!" Telling the story had really taken a toll on Ant.

"You wanna talk about what happened in court?" Preme asked.

"Yeah, I'll tell you, but maybe we should wait until later on, or maybe the weekend. The sun is about to come up and I'll have to get ready to do the feed and clean."

"Yeah, you're right. We'll get some rest and I'll cook us up something later. If you want, we can spin the yard tonight and kick it."

"Don't you have a program?" Ant asked. Preme began to chuckle and responded: "Of course I have a program. Doesn't everybody? But, for a crate of Newport's a week, I get checked in and accounted for."

"I guess money really does talk huh?" asked Ant…. "Like a muthafucka" replied Preme.

****

Two nights in a row, both Saturday and Sunday, Ant and Preme sat up all night talking. To be more exact, Ant talked while Preme listened. Staying up all night was starting to take a toll on them. When they finally decided to lay down and get some rest, Ant couldn't fall asleep right away. He found that talking about what happened had a two-fold effect on him: It was painful while he was telling it, but he felt so much lighter since he was letting it all out.

Ant had finally dozed off for about an hour, before he had to get up and complete his duties on the gallery. Once he was done with everything, he went back up and back to bed. He did the same thing that afternoon too. By the time Ant did the dinner feed-up, he was well rested. Once he was finished with all his duties for the evening, he went next door to Preme's cell. Preme had been up a couple of hours, and in that time, he had prepared food for both of them. Preme passed Ant his bowl and they stood there talking and eating.

"Yo, let's spin the yard a few times tonight" Preme said, even though he knew Ant didn't really like the yard, but Preme also knew that Ant needed to get used to being around people. After all, he was about to go back into the real world. "Man, you know I hate going to the yard. If I wanna stand around, I can do that in my cell. If I wanna watch T.V., I can do that in my cell."

"We won't be out there to stand around or watch T.V. If you want, we could put some work in on the weights, or we could just walk around and kick it; your call."

"Alright, let's hit the weights for a few. I haven't used the weights in a minute, so I won't be able to hang with you. Then we can spin a few times, but I don't want to talk about my past in the yard; I'd rather finish telling you up here like I have been." Preme nodded in agreement.

"That's cool, cause you never know who's listening." Ant went to his cell and got ready, and so did Preme.

Chapter 11

An hour later, Preme and Ant entered the already crowded yard. They made their way over to the weight pile, only to find that it was too crowded. But when the occupants saw Preme, room was quickly made to accommodate whatever he desired to use. Preme told Ant they'd do light chest work, thinking Ant would be able to handle at least 185 on the long bar. Preme quickly realized that Ant needed a spotter with just the quarters on. Preme encouraged him, and didn't let on to how surprised he was. One thing Preme noticed, was that all eyes seemed to be on them. Some inmates came by and spoke, but most just stood a ways off staring and whispering. He figured they were probably talking shit about Ant struggling with the weights.

They wrapped up the workout and decided to spin the yard. As they made their way around the yard, they could only make it a few steps without someone stepping to greet Preme. When they finally made it around once, they picked up speed and continued to walk. Ant was telling Preme about his musical influences and favorite artists, in both Gospel & secular music. As Ant was talking, Preme was trying desperately to figure out why all eyes were on them, as well as trying to pay attention to Ant. Preme heard Ant spit out names like Timothy Wright, Richard Smallwood, The Clark Sisters, Valerie Boyd, Stevie Wonder, Patti LaBelle, Oleta Adams & Al Green. Ant was going on and on, when someone called Preme.

"Yo Preme". Preme turned to see an old timer by the name of Magic coming his way. Magic was from Harlem and used to be the man on the pimp tip. Magic had been locked up now for about 25 years. Even now in prison,

Magic still had his hands on everything from selling drugs to both selling and fucking "boy pussy". Preme showed him respect by speaking when he saw him, based on the fact that he was from the Harlem world… but he wasn't Preme's cup of tea.

"What's poppin Magic?" Magic had to be at least 60, but you couldn't tell his old ass that he wasn't 30. He still sported a pair of gazelles from the early 90's and wore his pants hanging off his ass. The worst of it was when he opened his mouth, you were blinded by the gold… there was no white to be seen.

"Let me holla atcha' playa." Magic said.

"Give me a sec Ant" Preme said to Ant, who in turned nodded. Preme and Magic walked off a few feet away, and Magic turned and gave Ant a look that didn't sit right with him. But he didn't dwell on it. When Preme and Magic were several feet away from everyone, they stopped, and Magic got the conversation going.

"Yo, so what's up baby pa?" Asked Magic, whom you could not tell him he wasn't the epitome of cool.

"Same ole, same ole. So, what do you want to kick it about?"

"Yo, baby pa, you know me, and you know I'm always gonna keep it real with you, ya dig?

"I should hope so Magic. So, what's the deal? I got my son waiting." Magic studied Preme, while rubbing his salt & pepper goatee.

"That's what I wanted to kick it with you about; your son." When Magic said son, he used air quotations. "Word around, is that your fucking him." Preme could not believe the shit that was coming from this dude's mouth. Before he could regain his composure and speak, Magic continued on.

"They saying you don't come out cause you up on his gallery spending all your time with him. They also saying that all of a sudden, the kid has a T.V. and new gear. All I'm saying is, if it's true, when you're finished with him… can I tap that? That mother fucker got some pretty ass eyes and lips. I bet that "Pussy" tight too."

Before Preme even realized it, he had dead armed the old freak ass bastard, and it didn't stop there. Magic's old ass hit the floor and covered up, but Preme commenced to stomp him out and kick the living shit out of him. As Preme stomped fire out of Magic, he was yelling at him, giving him a verbal beating as well. "You sick freak ass bastard! This will teach your gay ass about spreading rumors. Take this back to all the bitch ass mother fuckers running their mouths!"

The situation quickly escalated, even though no one knew who threw the first blow. But when one person finally saw what was happening, it was like a chain reaction. Ant had been standing a little way up, looking at the T.V. with his back to Preme and Magic, when he noticed several inmates rushing past him and headed towards the area he last saw Preme. Before he could turn around to see what was going on, several CO's emerged from all over, running and screaming "Break it up!" When Ant turned, he couldn't see much cause a mob of inmates had enclosed the action. Ant tried desperately to see where Preme was, but it wasn't until the CO's were able to break up the mob, did Ant see Preme. The CO's had grabbed Preme in the midst of him kicking someone, and within seconds they had him on the ground, cuffing him. Ant was in a state of shock, and didn't realize he was moving towards the crowd. When he got closer, it was then that he saw Magic on the floor bleeding. Some of the CO's were tending to him, probably asking if he could walk and so forth. Just then, Preme was lifted from the ground by a pair of CO's and taken back to the facility.

As Preme was being led away, he searched the crowd, hoping to see where Ant was. He spotted him just ahead to his right, Ant looked at Preme and Preme gave him a slight smile, trying to assure him that he was okay. Ant just stood there and watched Preme pass by and go in to the building. A few minutes later, with the assistance of a couple of inmates and two CO's behind them, Magic started limping his way back to the building too... more than likely headed to the infirmary. When Magic saw Ant looking at him, he held his head down in shame. Ant just stood there, waiting for the early call back.

****

Ant raced up the steps that led to the gallery. Once he made it up there, there was a CO at the controls waiting to let him in. "You staying out until rec comes in Morgan?" asked the CO.

"Yea, I'm gonna straighten up the gallery."

"Alright, I'll leave your cell and the shower open. By the way, there's gonna be another keep-lock feed on the gallery. The fellow stays in the cell next to you. He probably won't take any food; he has a whole warehouse of food in his cell. I heard he has more money than God." Ant wished the CO would cut the convo short, open the gate and take his ass down stairs; Ant needed to see Preme.

Is was as if the CO read his mind. He opened the gallery gate so Ant could step in. "Close the shower when you're done, and make sure it's locked. I'll be downstairs." "Gotcha, thanks." Ant said, and he quickly walked down the tier towards his and Preme's cells. Ant walked straight past his cell, straight to Preme's. Preme was sitting on the bed, wearing nothing but a colorful pair of Joe boxer's, staring at the T.V.

"What the fuck was that all about?" Asked an out of breath and still excited Ant.

"You should really stop using language like fuck. It doesn't sound right coming out of your mouth. You're the Choir Boy, and your language should reflect such." Preme scolded. Ant couldn't believe this shit! Here he was trying to find out what caused Preme to stomp the old timer out, and instead, he was being scolded for his choice of words. Ant was furious.

"I'm 25-years-old. I think at this age, I can use any words I so desire."

"Yeah, yeah, you're grown and all that. I didn't say you couldn't use it. I said it doesn't sound correct coming out of your mouth… Choir Boy."

"Stop calling me that!" Ant yelled.

"You're always gonna be the Choir Boy, so you might as well get used to it. Besides, it's better than being called "Crack-head boy", "drug selling boy" or "thieving boy" … shall I keep going? Be grateful people only see a Choir Boy when they look at you."

"Whatever. Now, what was that all about, you and the old head?" Ant asked, quickly steering things back to the subject at hand.

"Nothing. Magic violated and I beat his old frontin' ass. Simple. Case closed."

"Case closed? Tell me what went down?"

"I told you it was nothing. I'm gonna make some sandwiches, you down?"

"Fuck a sandwich! It's amazing how I can tell you every detail of my life, the good, the bad and the ugly, and here you are holding out on me! Thanks friend!" With that, Anthony turned and walked into his cell. He quickly took his clothes off, wrapped a towel around himself and went to the showers.

While Ant was in the shower, he stood there letting the hot water mix with his tears. Ant was hurt, because despite all he had been through, he still had a loving heart. And as much as he tried to fight it, he cared about Preme. And even though Preme had said and done a lot of good things for him, the fact that he was withholding info from him hurt Ant. It hurt more than he thought possible.

While Ant was in the shower crying, Preme was in his cell kicking himself in the ass. He knew he had hurt Ant, and possibly lost his trust and friendship. All Preme wanted to do was spare Ant from any more pain; he really thought he was doing a good thing. Maybe, trying to do a good thing, isn't always the right thing.

****

Ant was back in his cell, after taking a 20-minute shower. He had just gotten dressed and was sitting on his bed, staring at the T.V., wondering what he was going to eat. He had plenty to choose from, thanks to Preme, whom he was determined not to talk to. He continued to just sit there. Meanwhile, Preme knew he had to make things right with Ant. So, while Ant was in the shower, Preme prepared turkey and cheese sandwiches for both of them. As he shredded the lettuce and sliced the tomato (using the lid from a can), he contemplated the situation with Ant. He realized Ant had been hurt enough, and trying to hide things from him, only added more hurt.

Also, Preme didn't like that people assumed Ant was gay, or him for that matter. Ant was simply a loner. He had manners and wasn't raised in the streets, so in this environment, that made him stand out. There are some who would say that what Shadrack did was Ant's fault, or even that he liked it. There are all kinds of sicko's out there, not just in the system. Preme wasn't concerned about what they said about him. He knew how to whip ass, and when it was all said and done, those mofo's were followers; whatever he did, everyone else copied. If people wanted to run their mouths and spread rumors, then fuck them. He didn't need any of them... but they sure as hell needed him!

Preme had just finished the sandwiches, when he heard Ant return from the showers. He figured he'd give him a few minutes to get dressed, and then he'd try like hell to repair damage he caused earlier. Preme waited ten minutes, then he knocked on Ant's wall. "Yo" a reluctant Ant answered. "Here" was Preme's response. Ant forced himself up from the bed, walked out of his cell and over to Preme's. When Ant got there, Preme handed him three sandwiches, and placed a can of BBQ flavored Pringles & 2 cans of Pepsi on the bars.

"Good looking. I was about to do the same." Ant said, who was about to turn and go back to his cell with the food.

"Yo Ant, before you go, I just wanted to..."

"Don't even worry about it, it's all good." Ant stated, cutting Preme off.

"Will you please let me finish? I apologize for not being up front with you. The reason I beat Magic's ass was because of something he said about you. I didn't want to tell you, cause I didn't want you to be upset. You've already been through enough, and I didn't want to add more on. Again, I apologize, and it won't happen again. That's my word." Ant stood there in a daze, trying to figure out what the hell the old dude had said about him that would make Preme go awol on him.

"What did he say?"

"First, are we still cool? Do you accept my apology?" Preme asked.

"Yeah, we cool. Ain't nothing change, as long as you keep in mind that I can handle shit. And don't treat me like a child."

"Got it. Like I said before, it won't happen again." Preme had hoped Ant wouldn't ask him again what Magic had said, but he had no such luck.

"So, what did he say?"

"You sure you want to know?" Preme asked reluctantly. "I'm gone" Ant said, and turned to head back into his cell. Preme reached out and grabbed Ant's arm.

"Alright, I'll tell you." Ant stopped and looked at Preme.

"What the fuck did he say?"

"You really need to stop using language like that, for real."

"Preme!" Ant barked, while looking extremely tired.

"He said he heard I was fucking you, and asked if he could get the left overs when I was done." Ant stood there listening, as both rage and hurt raced throughout his body. Tears filled his eyes, as the after math of Shadrack's abuse surfaced to present day. Preme stood there watching Ant, as he struggled with what he had just heard. "Ant. You have to always remember that there are a bunch of ignorant mother fuckers in this world, especially in this system. They hear bits and pieces of shit, and draw their own stupid conclusions. Fuck them! They don't know shit about you!" Ant was still, just standing there, listening to Preme talk about those bitches running their mouths. Ant needed to hear all that Preme was saying. Not that he didn't know it, he just needed to hear it again.

"All those bastards talking, would have never survived the shit you have. They'd be crackheads, homos... which most of them are anyway, without even going through what you did. Don't let that bullshit get to you. You're better than that... you heard?" Preme asked. Ant let Preme's words sink in... he knew he was right. People are gonna talk and run their mouths. Especially ignorant ones. However, there was still a part of him that wanted to knockout any and every one that had judged him without knowing him. Preme was right... FUCK THEM! Ant regained his composure, and was finally able to speak.

"You're right! But I have one question."

"What's that?" Preme said

"When you were breaking your foot off in his ass, did you tell him that half that ass whoopin' was from me?" Preme smiled and nodded his head.

"No doubt, I told him the entire ass kicking was from you! Cause if it was solely from me, there wouldn't have been a fight. I would've just killed the son of a bitch!"

Chapter 12

It was a few minutes before midnight when Preme and Ant took their positions close by the gate, with the mirror out. They had eaten, the CO did his count, and the gallery was quiet. Ant held the mirror and watched Preme pull on his blunt. Preme wasn't a regular weed smoker, he only smoked when he was stressed out… and that seemed to be more and more frequent. "I don't know how you can smoke that shit; it stinks." Ant stated with his face showing disapproval.

"This shit relaxes me; besides, I don't smoke it that often." Preme replied.

"That doesn't take away from the fact that it stinks."

"I'll make a deal with you."

"What's the deal?" Asked a curious Ant.

"I'll quit smoking altogether, if you stop cursing. Deal Choir Boy?" Ant thought about the offer, and figured, what the hell?!

"You got a deal." Preme got up from his seat at the gate, took the blunt and dropped it in the toilet. Ant watched through the mirror as Preme went to a stack of clothes piled on the floor and pulled out a single sock. It looked like it was stuffed with something. Sure enough, Preme reached inside and pulled out a zip loc bag filled with weed. He walked to the toilet, opened the bag and dumped it. Once the bag was empty, he flushed the toilet and watched it disappear. Preme returned to his seat at the gate and took the mirror from Ant. Ant just sat there looking dumb-founded. "I'm a man of my word, remember that. Now, let's pick up where you left off last night… whenever you're ready that is." Ant took a deep breath and began talking.

****

Ant sat on the old bus handcuffed and shackled to another young kid from the Bronx. Both were terrified as they crossed the bridge that led to Rikers Island, commonly known as the "Rock". Ant had heard way too many storied about this place, more than he cared to remember. Unfortunately, as he rode over the bridge, he remembered all of them; and he was petrified. As the bus came off the bridge and stopped at the entrance of the Island, Ant closed his eye and offered up a silent prayer that God would keep and protect him.

C-74, was a building on the "Rock" that housed all the adolescents. It was nicknamed "C-74 Adolescents at War". It housed the most notorious and the softest adolescent males in the five boroughs. There was more fighting, cutting, stealing and sexing going on in C-74 than all the other buildings on the Rock put together; and there were a lot of buildings. Ant was housed in Module 6 (a.k.a Mod. 6), along with 34 other young bucks. Mod. 6 was a 35-man dorm with a small recreation area, one 25-inch color T.V., five-bathroom stalls and five showers. There wasn't a day that went by that there wasn't some kind of drama in Mod. 6.

On Ant's first night there, he didn't sleep very well. The CO's hadn't brought the new arrivals to the dorm until almost midnight. At around 3:00 am, Ant got up to "pay a water bill" (to pee). It was dark in the dorm, and very bright in the bathroom, that the sudden change temporarily blinded him. He stumbled into the first stall he came to, and got the shock of his life. Right before him in the stall was a tall black kid, standing there getting head from a

Puerto Rican kid. Ant stood there, transfixed by what he saw. The crazy part was, they didn't even stop when Ant busted in. The black kid turned to Ant, and between a moan, spoke to him. "You want some son? He'll do you next or he can do us both at the same time, cause he's nice like that; right Culo? Ant didn't know much Spanish, but he did know that culo meant "ass". Culo, despite the stiff "piece of meat" in his mouth, responded with an "Mhm" to the black kid's question. Ant didn't open his mouth, he turned and fled back to his cube. Ant could not get the images out of his head from the stall. His mind wandered to all the times he had been pleased the very same way, and before day break, Ant had masturbated three times.

****

Less than 24-hours after being shot in the stomach, Shadrack was released from the hospital. Within days, with the assistance of his faithful wife Sylvia, he'd be back on his feet and back to his same old tactics. The rumor mill in the community and at Greater Second Chance Love Revival Tabernacle was buzzing nonstop. Word had spread like wildfire that Anthony shot Shadrack in his bedroom, and that Shadrack had been naked. It had also leaked out that Sylvia placed a robe on Shadrack, before calling the authorities. None of this phased Sylvia or Shadrack. When asked, they would simply say Anthony was controlled by Satan, had planned his actions, and that God would repay Anthony for his evil. They even went to the extreme to say how much they still loved him and would continue to pray for his deliverance.

There was also news that the late Mother Green's son had come to Anthony's aide. It was wide spread that Harold had showed up at Shadrack & Sylvia's house, just a few hours after Shadrack had been released from the hospital, demanding Anthony's belongings. Sylvia had answered the door, and once Harold stated the reason for his visit, she quickly shut the door. This infuriated Harold, who began yelling and beating on the door. Shadrack didn't have all his strength back from just being shot the day before, so he instructed Sylvia to call the cops. Even if Shadrack hadn't been shot and he had all his strength, he still wouldn't have gone head to toe with Harold. If it was any indication as to what Harold could do with his hands, based upon how he was pounding on the front door, Shadrack knew if he had gone out there his ass would be gravy!

The police had arrived, and while one talked with Shadrack and Sylvia, the other talked to Harold. The situation was resolved by asking Harold to leave and not return, which he reluctantly agreed to do. However, the neighbors had witnessed the entire event and quickly spread the word to those who weren't as fortunate. Some gave play by play accounts on their cell phones, to friends and family. All of this unwanted attention would come with a price. In the days following, Shadrack began receiving letters of members leaving his church. Key members, ones holding positions within the church, sent letters of resignation. Shadrack couldn't believe those bastards had left him behind with this bullshit. He wasn't concerned per say about the individuals who left, but rather their consistent offerings and about being able to say his church was filled. However, most of those who left, along with those who remained, all gave a $5,000 offering to the church's building fund two weeks prior. Those checks had cleared and was tucked nicely in the bank. Shadrack didn't doubt for one minute that the new members would eventually come; people couldn't resist him. There was a sucka born every minute! But for now, Shadrack had more pleasant things to focus on.

Shadrack would have the house all to himself for the next three days. Sylvia, had agreed over six months ago to speak at a women's conference in Daytona Beach, Fl. She was reluctant to leave Shadrack so soon, but he insisted. He was up and about with no problems… plus, he reminded Sylvia of the plumbing problem at the church that still needed to be tended to. With Sylvia gone, Shadrack had made some plans for the night. Peaches had called and said that he had merchandise from Prada, Gucci, and Shadrack's favorite; Armani. Shadrack had agreed to meet Peaches at the motel, where they had their last meeting. Peaches had called and said that he was at the hotel, in the same room waiting. Shadrack jumped in his car and took off to the motel.

As Shadrack drove, his mind went back to the last encounter with Peaches. He hoped this meeting would be just as eventful. Since the situation with Anthony, Shadrack hadn't thought sex until Peaches called. As he came off the expressway and came in view of the motel, he reached under the seat and grabbed the bottle of Remy that was left over from their last meeting. He parked in the small lot and quickly entered the room that Peaches was in. When Shadrack entered and closed the door, he noticed various suits, dresses and other goods throughout the room. The other thing that Shadrack noticed, was that Peaches was not alone. In the room with him was a young black male, who looked to be about 18. He was about 5'6, with smooth brown skin and long straight hair, pulled back into a ponytail. Shadrack had never seen this individual, but it was someone he hoped he'd get to know and see often.

Peaches let a few minutes pass, and then decided to get down to business. "Good evening Rev. This is my good friend and boosting partner Precious. Precious, this is the Rev. Shadrack E. Brown." Peaches said, playing the good hostess. Shadrack walked over to where Precious was standing, and extended his hand for him to shake, in which he did. Shadrack couldn't take his eyes off of Precious, but did manage to find words. "Well Precious, it is my pleasure and a very pleasant surprise to meet you tonight." "Nice meeting you Rev." said Precious, sounding like a 13-year-old girl, rather than a young adult male.

"Well Rev., we've got a great deal of stuff here; we hope you brought a lot of cash. And what's that you have there?" asked Peaches, taking the brown bag containing the Remy. Peaches quickly discarded the bag, opened it and took it straight to the head, then passed the bottle to Precious who did the same. For the next half-hour, Peaches & Precious showed Shadrack all the merchandise. They negotiated back & forth over prices, all while passing the Remy around. With majority of the deals settled, the three sat down on the bed to finish negotiating the price of a coach brief case and garment bag, which Shadrack really wanted, but didn't want to pay the $800 Peaches & Precious wanted for it. "Rev., we are letting it go for next to nothing; we could easily get $1,600 for this set. And, I didn't know Preachers drank" stated Precious, who had already been informed by Peaches, about how crooked Shadrack was.

"Well my dear Precious, even Jesus drank wine. But like I told Peaches, I only take a sip here and there, and only when I'm in the presence of such good company." Peaches who was tipsy and way too tired for Shadrack's bullshit tonight, knew it was time to get things rolling. "Look Shadrack, enough of your bullshit. The bags are going for $800, give us our fucking money so we can get out of here." Peaches was really getting tired of Shadrack, but he also had plans for him.

"Peaches, all I have left on me is a mere $500. I am willing to give you that and we can work a deal for the remaining money" Shadrack said with a pleading smile. "Shadrack, you've got more money than God, thanks to your congregation, so stop being so damn cheap. All monies have to be split. Precious boosted just as much of this shit as I did. So please, stop the madness. You don't want me to pull my blade out do you?" Peaches was walking back and forth in front of Shadrack, yelling at the top of his lungs, putting on a performance worthy of Broadway.

"Wait Peaches, let's see what kind of deal he's willing to make" said Precious, right on cue.

"Alright Rev., let's hear this deal." Shadrack took a moment, got up from the bed, looked at the two and said: "How long do we have the room for?"

"We have another 3 hours. Why?" Precious answered. Shadrack continued to pace, as if in deep though. "Well, I was thinking that I could be of service to both of you, being that we have three paid hours of room time."

"What the fuck does the mean, be of service?" Peaches asked. Shadrack got down on his knees in front of Peaches and began pulling on his zipper. When he released Peaches from the confines of his pants, he turned and looked back at Precious. "Feel free to get behind me and have your way." Precious got up from the bed, and before going over to violate Shadrack, he hit the record button on the camcorder hidden under a chair with a direct view of the bed, and Peaches watched Precious do it. As he sat there getting head from the Rev., Peaches wondered how exactly this video was going to be used against Shadrack and how it would help Anthony. Peaches didn't know Anthony personally, but read about the shooting in the papers, and it was the talk of the town. He didn't believe for one minute that Anthony was demon possessed or crazy. It was Precious' belief that the good Reverend had been taking sexual liberties with Anthony, and he just got fed up with it. After all, Peaches knew first-hand what the Rev. would do to an innocent young child. But this dog would have his day!

****

Ant had been on the Rock in Mod 6, building C-74 for almost eight months. Most of the dudes that had arrived with Ant from QHD, had gone upstate to complete their bids, and some even went home. But eight months after being there, Ant was still going to court and meeting with his lawyer.

The lawyer that Harold had hired for him seemed to be good and caring. He had listened intently as Ant bared everything that led up to him shooting Shadrack. The unfortunate part was, because there was no evidence of abuse, nor were there any complaints of Shadrack abusing other children, the D.A., nor the judge would allow or want to hear it. There seemed to be no way around it. The other unfortunate part was, Ant would certainly be doing some time. Mostly because his mother sided with Shadrack. A`nd because he didn't have any community support, the judge would have no choice but to send him away. It was the lawyer's job to get Ant the least amount of time possible; and his lawyer vowed to do just that.

Chapter 13

In the long months that Ant had been on the Rock, he had seen just about everything. He had witnessed cuttings, gang fights, fights over lovers, drug transactions and wars, prostitution, gambling and even a few ménages trois. He was even [involuntarily] a part of a riot. One Saturday, in the mess hall during lunch, they were serving beef patties. For some reason, beef patties always gave the youngsters an energy boost. Supposedly it all started over an argument about who the greatest rapper was; Biggie or Tupac. Mod 4 said Tupac and Mod 6 said Biggie. This argument was escalating for a few weeks now. Well, that Saturday, when Mod 6 got into the mess hall, Mod 4 was already seated. While Mod 6 was on the line getting their food, the Mod 4 crew began yelling shit like "Fuck Biggie", "Biggie's a snitch" and things along those lines. This caused Mod 6 to respond, saying "Tupac's a bitch", "That niggas a dick rider" and so on. By the time Mod 6 was seated, the tension was so thick you could cut it with a knife.

Ant sat there, taking his time eating his two patties. Trying to savor them, because dinner was a long time away and it was gonna be trash anyway. All of a sudden, in the midst of Ant taking a bite, a dude from Mod 4 yelled "Biggie ain't shit, Nas is better than that fat ass nigga". And before Ant knew it, all hell broke loose. Dudes were flying across tables, trays and food was being slung everywhere. Ant sat right there eating his patties, watching the action and was even able to grab a few patties before they were used as torpedo's. By the time the CO's were able to restore order, Ant had a full stomach and was thankful that he yet again escaped untouched.

****

It was sentencing day for Ant, and the court room was packed with media and folks just being plain nosey. With the exception of Harold, his wife Denise and possibly the lawyer, no one was there out of sheer concern for Ant, and he was well aware of it. Ant turned his attention to Sylvia who was on the stand, expressing why Ant shouldn't be shown any mercy. *"I raised my son to be a God-fearing young man, but somehow along the way, the devil got a hold of him."* A collective gasp was heard throughout the courtroom. It was unclear as to whether the people were shocked at the "truth" she told about her son, or how incredibly stupid and foolish she sounded.

Ant looked over at Harold and Denise, who were visibly astonished by Sylvia's performance. Sylvia even dressed the part, in a simple Donna Karen jacket and shirt, a white silk blouse, no jewelry, other than the two karat diamond studs in each ear. No makeup and her hair was swept back over her shoulders. Ant was still watching Harold and Denise when he saw Harold shake his head in disgust. Harold looked up and caught Ant watching him. As if summoned, Denise looked over at Ant. The two of them placed smiles on their faces, hoping it would reassure Ant of their love and support. It seemed that Ant got the message and smiled back. He then turned his attention back to Sylvia, who seemed to be finished. *"I believe that giving him the maximum sentence would be the best thing for him. Hopefully it will save his life. It hurts to know that he did this to a man that loved and still loves him as his own. If you want to help Anthony judge, then give him the maximum sentence."* With a lowered head, Sylvia had finished.

"Is there anything else you desire to add Mrs. Brown?" the judge asked. "There is nothing left to add your honor."

"Well, before you step down, I have some questions that I need you to answer in order to help me make my decision" said the Judge Winston L. Meyers. Judge Meyers, looked like he was pushing 70 years of age. He had a head full of white hair, horned rimmed glasses and more spunk than a 20-year-old. *"Fine your honor, anything I can do to help"* an eager to please Sylvia responded, as she shifted in her seat.

"Tell me, Mrs. Brown, is it true that Anthony maintained a perfect grade point average?" Sylvia was not prepared for this type of questioning, and looked to the D.A. for help. The D.A. caught the look and jumped up. "Your honor, with all due respect, I really don't see any relevance in asking about Anthony's GPA; he's a menace to society…" The judge waved his hand, cutting the D.A. off and sat up in his chair.

"This is MY courtroom. It is not your job to see the relevance, as you so put it; it's my job. That's the reason I'm sitting here and you're sitting down there. Not another word, or you'll be sitting in jail for contempt." It was clear that the judge was furious. He sat there staring at the D.A. until he took his seat. "Now, Mrs. Brown… answer the question."

"I really don't recall, your honor, what exactly his average was" responded a clearly nervous Sylvia, who looked down at Shadrack who sat there expressionless.

"Mrs. Brown, I really cannot believe that you do not know your only child's scholastic average. Now, I'm going to say this one time and one time only. Please answer my questions, and do not, I repeat, DO NOT play games with me in my court room. I'm waiting for my answer." The judge leaned back in his chair, crossed his arms across his chest, and awaited Sylvia's answer. Sylvia nervously smoothed the lapels of her jacket and finally began to speak.

"I reckon he did indeed have a perfect average."

"You reckon? I'll log that as a yes. But from here out, let's simplify the situation by you answering yes or no. Let's move forward." The judge looked as if he could get his hands around Sylvia's neck, he'd be going to jail. "Now, is it true your son was made a part-time manager at Western Beef. The youngest part-time manager in the stores history?"

"That is true your honor." Sylvia said, who seemed agitated by the judge's public reprimand.

"I told you, a simple yes or no is all that I require. I'm not going to tell again Mrs. Brown. I'm really starting to wonder, what type of environment you and the Rev. Brown over there actually provided for Anthony." This time, it was Sylvia's turn to fold her arms across her chest and roll her eyes, the way a teenage girl would do. If the judge saw that, he definitely let it slide, and proceeded with his questions: "Is it also true, that Anthony is a self-taught, accomplished musician and vocalist?"

"Yes"

"Is it true, that Anthony made quite a name for himself singing at church functions throughout the Tri-State area?"

"Yes"

"Mhm… I find it hard to believe that this same young man, who as you put it "is under the influence of the devil"."

Judge Meyers replied, as he shuffled some papers on his desk, until he found the one he wanted. He studied it for a few seconds, then put it back down and turned his attention back to Sylvia. "Mrs. Brown, do you love your son?"

"How could a mother not love her child?!"

"Please scratch that answer from the record. Mrs. Brown will answer in the manner in which I instructed." Judge Meyers was fit to be tired and everyone in the courtroom knew it. "We all await your answer."

"Yes"

"And, you believe that sending your son away for 25 years, a man's sentence… will be beneficial to him? Mind your response Mrs. Brown."

"Yes!" The reporters in the courtroom couldn't wait to get out of there and write their stories. They could probably milk this story for at least a week, just talking about Sylvia's testimony alone!

"Have you been to see your son?" the judge continued.

"No"

"I will allow you to give more than a yes or no answer on this last question. Why haven't you been to see him?" The courtroom was so quiet that it's quite possible everyone was holding their breath. Sylvia sat straight up, looked at Anthony and responded:

"Because, light has no fellowship with darkness."

Many in the courtroom gasped at Sylvia's response, as several reporters jumped up and ran for the exit, eager to get this story in print. Judge Meyer's sat there, looking unbelievably at Sylvia. He shook his head in apparent disgust, and then he spoke: "You're excused Mrs. Brown. We'll reconvene after lunch, at 1:15 pm." Sylvia stepped off the stand to an awaiting Shadrack, who took her arm and they both proceeded to the exit, with their heads held high.

****

"All rise." Everyone was back in their places, and stood as Judge Meyers entered the courtroom, took his seat, adjusted himself until he was comfortable and then thundered "Be seated." It seemed that there were even more people in the courtroom that afternoon then there was that morning. Word must've gotten out that this case was more entertaining than an MC Hammer concert. *"I've had the opportunity to review several letters written in support of Anthony Morgan."* Judge Meyers said, as he gathered several papers from a folder on his desk and studied them as he continued to talk. *"There are several from Anthony's teachers, both past and present, who all express the great potential of this young man."* The judge grabbed another pile of papers. *"There are numerous letters from employee's at Western Beef, who describe Anthony as being a trustworthy, hardworking and diligent young man."* Sylvia and Shadrack sat there stoned faced and unmoved.

"I have one from Harold Greene, who's late mother took a special interest in Anthony I'm told. I also have several from members, well more than likely, former members of Greater Second Chance Love Revival Tabernacle, where the Brown's serve as pastors. It's really quite amazing that with a name like that, there seems to be so little love from the Brown's to Anthony." The judge paused to let that sink in. *"I believe these letters speak volumes about Anthony, and despite what the D.A. and the Brown's have stated*

about Anthony, I don't believe that giving him the maximum sentence is warranted. Anthony, would you please stand?" Anthony slowly rose out of his seat and stood tall and erect, as if this was the moment he had been waiting for. But inside, he was scared for his life. The judge was taking his time, and Ant just wished he'd get it over with. After what seemed like forever, the judge started again.

"Anthony. First, let me say that I appreciate your honesty. You don't find that very often from a young man of your age. Secondly, I believe in my heart that there were serious reasons that led up to you doing the things you did." The judge looked over at Shadrack, who immediately turned his head slightly so he wouldn't be eye to eye with the judge. Then Judge Meyers turned his attention back to Anthony. "Unfortunately, I am unable to address whatever those things were. Hopefully all of that will come out and will be dealt with in the near future." Judge Meyers took his glasses off and rubbed his eyes, as if he was tired. He placed his glasses on the desk and with what seemed like a great effort, he began once again: "You are before me, because you illegally purchased a fire-arm and then shot your step-father. Regardless if your actions were warranted, it's still a crime." The judge looked over once again at Shadrack, who still refused to look at the judge. Meanwhile, the spectators

in the courtroom were loving the show that was going forth. The media would have chosen to be in attendance here, then lying on a beach in the Cayman Islands… that's just how entertaining and intense the atmosphere was.

"Once again, I don't believe that giving you 25 years is going to help you. Fortunately, we've been given a new sentencing guideline, and you'll be the first person that I use it on. I am sentencing you to a flat 12 years, which *means you'll do 10, and when your sentence has been completed, you will be released. You will not have to go before the Parole Board, nor will you be on parole when you're released. I have combined both the weapons charge and the attempted murder charge together. I've taken your age into consideration; you will be 25 -years-old when you're released... with a new start and an entire life ahead of you. I advise you to learn all you can and to keep in contact with those who have shown their love and support towards you. Feel free to write this court if you have any questions, and... I will be checking on you. That is all; this court is adjourned."*

Ant stood there, knowing that he had been shown mercy, but he couldn't fathom doing 10 years in prison. Ant's thoughts were interrupted by the voice of his lawyer and the presence of Harold and Denise. "We did better than I thought we would; we were lucky to have Judge Meyers." As the lawyer spoke, the guards quickly came and handcuffed Ant. As soon as he was cuffed, they began leading him out the courtroom. Ant looked back at Harold and Denise, who stood by his lawyer. They gave him encouraging smiles, which Ant tried to return. "Hang in there; we'll get through this together." Harold yelled out. Ant turned his attention to the guards who led him out of the courtroom, into the waiting elevator. As Ant rode in the elevator, a depression came over him like a flood... ending it all, seemed like the only option now. The only question was... how would he do it?

****

Four days after his sentencing, Ant went to the CO and requested his razor, so he could shave. The CO gave it to him and went back to playing with his electronic hand held game. The dorm was quiet, because everyone was in the yard. Ant took the razor and sat in one of the stalls in the bathroom. He just sat there, looking at the razor and at his wrist. The demonic force of suicide was riding Ant, and it was refusing to let go. Ant took the razor, placed it on his wrist and slowly ran it across the middle. An incision was made, that quickly produced blood. Ant quickly did the same thing to the other wrist. Ant sat there as the blood steadily began to flow and fall. As he sat there, he began to doze off. But right before he blacked out completely, he heard a faint scream way off in the distance. Culo slept in that day and hadn't gone to the yard, because he was up all night the night before performing service for a few of the guys in the dorm. He had woken up with a full bladder that badly needed emptying. He walked into the bathroom and saw blood on the floor coming from one of the stalls, where he also spotted a pair of legs. Culo knew immediately what was happening. Before he could run to get a CO, there was a loud thump inside the stall. Ant had fallen off the stool and onto the floor. Culo couldn't move, but he let loose a scream that made the CO drop his game and come running!

<u>Chapter 14</u>

Both Ant and Preme sat quietly. Ant didn't know if he was quiet because he was tired of talking, or because it still hurt to rehash all that mess. He was willing to bet that it was the latter. Preme on the other hand, knew why he was quiet. He couldn't fathom the stuff he had just heard over the last few hours. In Preme's mind, this was the type of madness you saw on a Sunday night HBO movie; this shit didn't really happen in real life. At least not to anyone he knew… and they survived to talk about it. Still, after hearing Ant talk about his past, Preme found it extremely hard to find something to say once Ant got quiet. Ant had demanded that he not try to spare his feelings and treat him like the man he was, so Preme began asking the questions that was on his mind.

"You really wanted to end it all huh?"

"I was just so sick and tired of the bullshit…"

"Hey, we had a deal remember? No more cussin." Preme interrupted, sounding like the old folks from the country by saying "cussin".

"Yeah, you're right… my bad" replied Ant, as he made a mental note to cut the profanity. The funny thing was, Ant never liked hearing profanity, let alone using it, but it was something he did to fit in. He'd never forget the night he went to South Road to buy the gun and Midnight made fun of him for using the term "cheddar". From that night on, Ant tried not to standout and tried hard at being "common". It never seemed to work though, but that didn't stop him from trying. However, since meeting Preme, he no longer felt that he had to be someone he wasn't in order to be accepted. Ant began to realize that is was okay to have an identity of his own. That by being a bi-product of the masses, just to have people around you, was the coward way. Ant often thought about all the gang members that he had come across over the last nine plus years. The majority of them, if not all of them, were afraid of being his own man.

The awakening came after Preme had the fight with Magic. Preme had stated how people talk without knowing the facts. He said they don't know shit, so fuck 'em. "I was sick and tired of all the drama, the hurt & pain. I just felt like, enough was enough." "Do you still feel like that at times?" Preme was curious to hear Ant's response to that. He really hoped Ant was not still suicidal. "There are times that I get depressed and I'm haunted by what happened, but not to the point that I want to check out."

"Why do you think you just wanted to kill yourself just that one time and no other?" Preme knew some would laugh at his choice of questions, but he had heard so many stories of suicides and attempted suicides, even stories of family members that made him really want to understand. "I never said I never wanted to end it all no other time; I said I only acted on it that one time." Ant stated, setting the record straight. "So, you've thought about ending it a lot?"

"Suicide is a spirit; a demonic force that's addictive like drugs. I've never experienced drugs, but from what I've read and seen, drugs and suicide are about the same. That spirit and addiction of suicide are more powerful than any drug addiction." Ant had never spoken of these beliefs to anyone, but he felt so at ease with Preme that things just came out naturally. "So, how were you able to break the addiction. Did you go to S.A. meetings…. Meaning Suicide Anonymous?" Ant didn't respond to the S.A. joke, and Preme wanted to kick himself for trying to make light of such a heavy issue. However, Preme had his own reasons and skeletons for trying to do so. He hoped Ant wouldn't hold it against him. Ant proceeded as if he didn't hear it.

"It took a lot of prayer, even fasting, and it still does. It's not an easy spirit to shake."

"What you're telling me is, prayer and not eating, helped you conquer suicide?" Preme asked unbelieving.

"Yeah, that's exactly what I'm saying."

"Despite all the hell you had to go through, you remained strong in your faith in God?" The sun would be coming up soon, and Preme was tired, but he had to get some answers… otherwise he wouldn't be able to go to sleep. "No, I didn't always have or keep my faith in God. Had I been consistent in my faith, I wouldn't be in prison. I would have left it to the Lord to work it out." Before Ant could go on, Preme jumped back in with a vengeance.

"You went through hell from the age of seven until you were fifteen; that's eight long ass years… eight fucking years! You're gonna sit there and tell me that you wouldn't have done what you did if you had kept your faith?"

"That's EXACTLY what I'm saying."

"That sick, frontin', triflin' ass dude hurt you for all those years, and you would have just continued to allow it to happen? Tell me that's not what you're saying." Preme was getting very worried and couldn't wait to hear his response.

"That's not what I'm saying. Keep in mind, that I was 15, in school and I had a job. I should have continued to dodge him and wait on the Lord to serve vengeance."

"I hear that, but ain't that much dodging and waiting in the world." Preme said, with a smirk.

"I felt like that many times, myself. But then my mind would take me back to that night I sung at the church and Mother Green came to me afterwards with that message." Ant paused and reflected back to that night. Preme was anxious for Ant to keep going, but knew how much he loved Mother Green and how her passing affected him. "You alright?" Preme asked.

"Yeah, it's just so amazing. She said that God was with me, and that he would bring me through. She told me that He sees and cares, and that He had not forgotten me. When I look back now, at what transpired... how could I not serve a God like that?"

"Well Ant... you're better than me."

"No, I'm not. I just realized that God is always at work, even when we don't think He is. Not getting immediate results when we want is a hard pill to swallow. Especially when we are being done wrong. But, knowing that it will indeed work out for our good, sure does help." Preme sat there quietly, thinking about all Ant had just expressed. It sounded good, but things didn't work out for the good in his life. And not the lives of his family. Preme wasn't about to wait for the Lord to serve vengeance. At the first opportune moment, upon his release; Preme knew he'd be the one to serve judgement to the deserving. "I know you're sincere in what you've expressed, but it's a lot for me to just grasp because you said it. I really need to think on all of this. Maybe, one day I'll get there... but I don't foresee it." Preme stopped himself, for he didn't want to shift the focus onto him... because, he wasn't ready to answer any personal questions.

"Well, it sounds as if you have some issues with some folks. I won't ask now, but trust me... it's not worth it. The penalty is far greater than the revenge itself." Ant said. "I hear that, but you know there are people out there who've had it worse than you. With that being said, imma go to bed. More than likely, they'll be here real early with my ticket for the fight." And with that, Preme got up from his spot and laid down on his bed. He just laid there staring at the ceiling. Ant sat there wondering what Preme meant by his last statement. Ant wondered if Preme was referring to himself. With stiff limbs, Ant forced himself up from his spot. He quickly laid on his bed, tired and in need of a nap, before his gate opened for work. A nap just didn't seem possible though, for Ant had so many questions running through his mind that he needed answers to. Like, who is Preme really. And what is he hiding? Ant didn't think Preme was being dishonest, but rather… not being forthright about himself. It was apparent that Preme was battling demons of his own. But what were they?

Anthony had just under three months to his release. He hoped that within that time, Preme would open up and just trust him. Before Ant nodded off, his mind remembered a line from an old Debarge song that said "It will reveal in time." And found that to always be true, so he didn't think that this situation with Preme would be any different. A minute later, Ant was softly snoring.

****

Ant awakened about 20 minutes before his cell was scheduled to open for work. He quickly got up, said a quick prayer of thanks, and then went to the sink to handle his business. When his cell did open, he looked down the gallery and saw that the feed-in trays had arrived. Ant went about his routine as usual, feeding the keep-locks, picking up the garbage, and overall making sure the gallery was spotless. Ant looked in on Preme who was laying on his back, mouth open and knocked out. As Ant turned and left

Preme's cell to finish his morning tasks, he wondered if today would be the day that his questions pertaining to Preme would be answered. He quickly dismissed the thought, because he knew Preme would insist that he finish his story before they got into his.

Ants mind then shifted into an entirely different direction. He began thinking about his future and what awaited him upon his return to society. He had still yet to make up his mind where he was going to live. Harold and Denise had made him two different offers. They had invited him to stay with them in Texas for as long as he wanted, or he could stay in the home that Mother Green had lived in. Harold had never sold the house, knowing that his mother would want Anthony to have it. Ant was grateful for Harold and Denise, because they stuck by him when no one else would... not even his own mother. However, Ant couldn't see moving into their home. Especially since their children were grown and already out of the house. The only logical thing to do was stay at Mother Green's, and prayerfully he would find a job.

Ant had managed to finish his schooling and received his GED during his first year of incarceration. Before college was taken out of the New York State Prison System, Ant had managed to earn his Bachelor's Degree in Business. He figured, if push came to shove, he could always return to Western Beef until something better came along. Many of the employees who worked there when he did were still there... but in better positions. Every Christmas, for the last ten years, Western Beef would send him a 35 lb. package and a $50 money order. Ant was grateful for them! He never spent one cent of those $50 money orders. Instead, he sent them to Harold, and he put them in the bank for him. Ant knew nothing on the outside was cheap, but he knew he would be able to get by for a bit with his savings. Another thing that was constantly on his mind was women. He tried hard to keep the spirit of lust under wraps. Through prayer and fasting, he was able to overcome masturbation... and that alone was a miracle. There were times [since being locked up] that he found himself masturbating up to five times a day! Usually he'd end up doing it three times a day, but sometimes three just didn't cut it.

Ant wondered if he would ever get married and have children of his own. There was a time, many years ago, when he thought Renee would be his wife and they would have a load of kids. He often wondered about Renee and how she was doing. After he got arrested, he knew for sure he'd hear from Renee, but that dream eventually faded. One memory that Ant tried desperately to not think about was the loss of his unborn child. Ant didn't want his child, or any child, to be subjected to the madness in which he was forced to endure. But despite knowing that... it still wasn't an easy reality to face. Ant was always told that time will heal all wounds; but not in his case.

****

Later that day, after all the trays and garbage from lunch had been collected, Ant had to help someone move to the annex again. This was one of the parts of his job that he really hated, due to the fact that he had no choice but to walk throughout the facility and come into contact with people. The move went forth uneventful, and Ant wasn't mad at that. He had expected comments and stares because of the fight between Preme & Magic. But as far as he could tell, there were none... and Ant was grateful. He finally made his way down the gallery to his cell, when he saw Preme's arms resting on his cell bars. Often times inmates, including Ant, found themselves standing in that very same position, lost in thought. Preme must have woken up after Ant left to help with the move, thought Ant. "What's happenin playa? I thought you would still be knocked out for at least another hour or two." Ant asked, catching Preme completely off-guard, causing him to slightly jump when he heard Ant's voice.

"First off, don't call me playa. Do I look like a playa to you? If anything, I'm the mutha fuckin coach… remember that. Secondly, I would still be asleep, but the jerk woke me up to serve me with this bogus ass ticket" stated Preme, as he grabbed a yellow piece of paper from the bed and handed it to Ant. The yellow paper, or ticket as Preme called it, is known as a "misbehavior report." In the NYS prison system, when an inmate violates a rule, the CO's or civilian employees can write a misbehavior report and a hearing is held to determine innocence or guilt. There are three types of misbehavior report that are broken down into tiers. A Tier I, is a minor infraction and will get you no more than a couple of weeks loss of recreation. Tier II and III are more serious. If you are found guilty of a Tier II, you can spend up to a maximum of 30 days in keep-lock, loss of commissary, packages, phone use, and will be charged a $5.00 fine. If you are found guilty of a Tier III, you lose all your "privileges", charged a $5.00 fine, and you could be confined to the hole for years.

Ant took the ticket and quickly looked to see what Tier it was; he knew there was no way it was going to be a Tier I. He was afraid it would be a Tier III, due to the fact that the fight took place in the yard, and they take those very seriously… due to all the gang violence. However, to Ant's surprise, it turned out to be a Tier II. Ant then looked for the charges, which simply said "Fighting". That was also good, because they could have put more charges on him.

Seeing as how about 98% of the reports written were usually lies. Ant quickly read the brief report, which basically stated that Cecil Brown (which Ant concluded to be Preme's government name) was fighting with one Xavier Jackson, an elderly inmate. All in all, that was the meat of the report; Preme was looking at possibly 30 days.

"Cecil Brown, huh?" Ant said to Preme with a smile.

"Don't even play son, it's Preme." Preme stated with no real conviction.

"I like that name, but how about I just call you CB?" Ant could no longer contain his laughter, and he didn't even try to. Preme didn't even respond, he just looked at Ant with piercing eyes that said "that's enough". Ant quickly tried to compose himself. He knew from being in the system all those years just how sensitive cats could be about their real names. "Okay, my bad. I was just playing." Ant stated, still trying to get himself in control again.

"Whatever" Preme responded.

"Yo, you came off good! This is only a Tier II, so they can't give you no more than 30 days across the board." Ant said.

"I'll go to the hearing on Thursday, and get 15 days keep-lock."

"How do you know that?" A curious and bewildered Ant asked.

"Because I bought the 15 days." Preme responded with a smile that showed all the expensive metal and jewels in his mouth.

"I don't understand."

ChoirBoy

"Ant, it's time you stop being so naive. Yes, even those who call themselves "correcting" us can be bought." Preme was in teacher mode, and was ready to school his student on the facts of life.

"How much did 15 days cost you?" Ant asked, still somewhat dumbfounded.

"Well, I had 52 packs of cigarettes in here this morning, and now I only have 2; you do the math." Ant scratched his head in amazement, still trying to comprehend what he was just told. Despite all Ant had experienced and been subjected to, he realized that there was still so much he had yet to learn. "Well, I'm still kinda tired, so I'm gonna lay down until around dinner time. What are you going to do?" Ant asked.

"I'm gonna fall out for a few too. When I get up, I'm gonna cook up something proper... you know how I do." Ant nodded and went into his cell. 50 packs of cigarettes for a 15-day sentence; Wonders never ceased to amaze Ant.

****

Preme had told Ant that he was going to take a nap before cooking, but he didn't think sleep was possible. Preme was one of those individuals who constantly stayed occupied to keep his mind from wandering. There were so many things that he wished never came back across his mind; unfortunately, that was impossible. As he laid there, Preme was oblivious to the various noises that were going on, on the block. TV's blasting, people yelling and someone was blasting Lil Kim's "La Bella Mafia" Cassette. Preme was so engrossed in his thoughts, that none of the sounds made it to his brain. No one would think or believe that Cecil Brown, a.k.a Preme, had demons of his own.

People looked at him and saw the money, the businesses, the clothes, his looks, and all the other attractive things about him, and thought he was all good. Little did they know, Preme worked hard to portray that to people. Unlike Ant, there were some things that Preme didn't think he'd ever be able to share with anyone; some things just hurt way too bad, and cut way too deep.

Being 27 years old, Preme had grown up with Hip-Hop music. He remembered his first Hip-Hop record, King Tim III, and living only blocks away from Apollo Theater, Preme always had access to all the shows. One of Preme's favorites was Tupac. As he laid there, he thought of the unjust plagues that had swept through him and his forever gone family. He thought of the person responsible and a line from one of Tupac's songs came to mind: "I ain't no killer, but don't push me, revenge is the sweetest joy next to getting pussy." Preme had plenty of women in his 27 years, but he'd see if what Tupac said was indeed true.

****

It was just after midnight; the CO just completed his nightly count and walk. Ant and Preme sat in their spots by the gate, with the mirror out. They had decided that they wouldn't break day tonight; by 1:00 am, they both planned on being in the bed. Ant had stated that he needed to get at least one full night's sleep during the course of the week. While Preme claimed that he had a few letters to write. Preme wasn't about to write anyone, but his mind was just so occupied with his own madness and plots of revenge, that he couldn't focus on Ant tonight... his mind really needed a breather.

Preme had really come to care for Ant, and if he couldn't give him his full attention while he was sharing the horrors of his life, due to his own, he'd rather wait until he could.

Ant, on the other hand, was wondering if this was a good time to see if Preme would answer some of his questions. Ant decided that there was only one way to find out. "Preme, how old are you?"

"Why?" Preme questioned, in response to Ant's question… Ant was caught completely off-guard by Preme's response.

"Just curious"

"I turned 27 two months ago."

"Are you married?"

"No." Preme answered with a raised eyebrow.

"Do you have any kids?"

"What the hell is this? 20 questions?" An agitated Preme asked in response. In a way, Ant was taken back by Preme's response and attitude. But a part of him expected Preme to respond in such a manner. Preme's response only confirmed that he had some demons of his own. Ant had to make sure he chose his words wisely.

"No, it's just that I don't know anything about you. You have done so much for me in such a short time, and I've opened up to you because I was under the impression that we're friends…" before Ant could go on, Preme cut in.

"And we are friends. I'd give you my right arm if you needed…" This time Ant cut in.

"Then why are you getting uptight because I'm trying to get to know you?" Ant's voice became that of a pleading eight-year-old, begging for attention from his father against the Sunday afternoon football game. Preme understood what Ant was expressing. However, he just wasn't ready to open up and share his demons. Preme knew he had to say something that would get Ant to back off a bit, but at the same time, not make him think he was hiding, holding out, or didn't trust him.

"I understand what you're saying, and you're right. It's just that I've never had any real friends. Everyone who claimed to be "my friend" was only there because of what I've got, or because of what they think/thought they could get from me. This is all new to me. Feel me?"

"Yeah, I feel you. I just thought you was trying to get in my head for whatever reason, and then break out." Responding, and always honest Ant. "Look Ant, I would never, ever do that. Like I said a few minutes ago, I'm new at this friendship thing. Believe me when I tell you, it has nothing whatsoever to do with you; it's me. I'm gonna tell you all about myself, after you finish your story… I just don't want to confuse the two." Ant sat there listening and believing that which Preme was stating. Ant didn't know what it was that made him trust and believe Preme… he hadn't trusted anyone in years. Not since Harold and Denise. Maybe, this was God showing him that everyone is not the same. That there are still some good people in the world. Ant continued to sit there in silence. It was Preme that continued on in hopes that Ant was not put off by his guarded ways.

"Plus, you're going home soon. Sooner than me by a bit, and I'm trying to learn all I can. That way I'll know the best ways in which I can help you. I know you have Harold and Denise, but you have me too. I plan on doing my part in making sure that you're alright and not wanting for anything when you walk out of here. Follow what I'm saying?" Preme asked, hoping he hit home with Ant. "You've already done enough; you don't have to do anything for me. In the short time that I've known you, you have done more for me than others." Ant didn't need to call names, and Preme already knew the "others" he was referring to. "Check this out. I know I don't have to do anything other than stay black, stay rich and die, but I want to help you and I'm making it my responsibility. So, in a way I guess I have to do this. Does that make any sense to you?"

"Yeah, I guess so." Responded Ant, again, sounding like a child instead of a 25-year-old man who was just about to complete a 10-year prison sentence. "Rest assured, you're gonna know everything there is to know about me. Most of it, you'll wish you didn't know. But I'm sure some of it has already passed your ears a time or two." Ant looked at Preme as if he didn't know what he was talking about. "Don't look at me like that. Even the CO's know I grew up hustling and slinging weight. So if they know... so do you. Am I right?" "I may have heard a thing or two, but I don't believe everything I hear. The very same ones who will tell a lie on you today, will be the same ones to tell one on me tomorrow."

"You can say that again. I'm glad to see that your learning" stated Preme, complimenting Ant on his new found awareness. "It doesn't take me long my man... it doesn't take me long." It was now 1:30 am, and they had both planned to be off the gate at 1:00. Ant yawned and they both realized that they had stayed up longer than they had originally stated, but it was time to get some much-needed rest. "Looks like someone's sleepy" Preme teased.

"Yeah, I can't even front" Ant stated, as he rubbed his eyes.

"Go get some rest. I'll holla at you later on." They both got up from the gate and each one laid out on his bed. Ant immediately began dozing off, while Preme's mind began to wander. He began to think about truths revealed regarding his long-gone family members; some whom he's never met. He began to reminisce about being raised in foster care, which for the most part, was worse than living on the streets… which he did from the age of 12 until he got on. Preme's mind went back to a dead mother who over-dosed when he was just 10-months-old, and an 11-year-old brother that committed suicide when Preme's mom was 8 months pregnant with him.

As Preme laid there thinking on all of this, emotions surfaced and weighed him down like tons of steel. A tear slid down Preme's right cheek. Crying was something he did on the regular, now that he was an adult. For many years, while he was a child, Preme cried often because of loss and because of his circumstances. But when he turned to the streets, crying was not acceptable. Now, like tonight, he welcomed the tears and allowed them to flow freely. Had all this not befallen him, Preme wondered what he could have become in life. What heights he could have reached. Somewhere out there, someone was responsible for the loss of his family, and for the tears he was now shedding. Preme knew who that someone was, and if it was the last thing he ever did… they would pay! Boy, would they pay!!

Chapter 15

T he next few days passed by uneventful. Preme went to his hearing and got 15 days just like he said... and other than that, everything was the same. It was Friday, Ant had completed his morning duties, and was now locked in his cell, laid back listening to Patti LaBelle's "Burnin" cassette. The CO was running keep-lock showers, and that was the reason Ant was locked in his cell. Mondays, Wednesdays & Fridays were the days they could shower, and they would be let out one by one for ten minutes. As Patti began wailing on "Release Yourself", Ant sat up and began grooving to the funky beat. Ant had played this cassette at least a thousand times, but each time he played it, it was like hearing it for the first time. There was only one other recording that came close to making him feel like that, and that was Oleta Adams "Evolution" recording. That cassette, he only played at night when everyone was asleep, for he often shed tears while listening to that one.

While Ant was grooving, he saw Preme pass by his cell, hair out in a fro, heading for the shower. Preme was the final keep-lock, so Ant threw his boots on because he knew his cell would be opening once Preme was back in his cell. Ant continued to groove with Patti. In the middle of "When You've Been Blessed", Preme passed back by and entered his cell. The second Preme's door locked, Ant's cell immediately opened. Ant walked up the gallery to see if there was anything that needed to be tended to. He found a puddle of water outside the showers, so he grabbed a mop and got rid of it. Once he returned the mop, he made his way back down the gallery to Preme's cell, figuring he would be dressed by now. When Ant reached Preme's cell, he found him sitting on the bed picking his afro. "What's good this morning Ant?" Preme asked cheerfully when he looked up and noticed Ant. "Ain't nothing. I see you decided to take it back to the 70's with the fro" Ant teased. Preme chuckled at Ant's tactics and replied:

"Naw, just wanted to wash it before I get it done again this afternoon."

"You do your own hair?" Ant asked, clearly amused at the possibility of Preme braiding hair; some things were just too hard to imagine.

"Hell no! I pay this chump from the Bronx to hook it up."

"So, how are you going to get it done this afternoon when you're still keep-locked?"

"You still haven't learned have you Ant? I thought we had established that money talks; CO Simmons up there, is no exception. After lunch, Easy will be over to hook the kid right on up. Ant stood there scratching his head in unbelief. The stuff one could do or get done when you have money, was amazing. Preme saw that Ant was tripping off this, even though he had told him time and time again what money can do. "One day, when your pockets are fat, you'll understand and see first-hand what I'm saying."

****

Just as Preme stated, right after lunch, CO Simmons opened the gate to allow a rail thin, tall, brown skinned kid onto the gallery. Ant was just coming out of his cell, about to go to Preme's when he saw the kid and stopped. Ant watched as he walked through the gate and proceeded down the gallery. While the kid was a ways off, Preme's cell opened. Preme came out of the cell with a bucket, which he placed down in front of the cell and sat on it. "I told you. Will you ever doubt the power of a dollar again?" Preme asked.

"Never." Ant answered, just as the kid reached them. "What up Preme?" The kid asked, making his presence known.

"Ain't nothing Easy. Easy... this my son..." Preme began introducing Ant, who was leaning on his cell bars a mere 3 ft. away, but was cut off by Easy. "Yeah, I know, this is "Choir Boy", the one you beat Magic up over."

"Don't start your shit Easy; you know how you Bronx cats are. And for the record, his name is Ant." Ant continued to lean on the bars and watch the exchange between Preme and Easy. From the statement Easy made about Preme beating up Magic over him, gave him an instant dislike for the kid. But Ant kept his mouth shut. After Preme corrected Easy on Ant's name, Easy [while getting his combs situated to start braiding] looked at Ant and said: "My bad, I thought Choir Boy was the name you went by." Ant still didn't say anything. He just nodded his head.

"Ant, get your bucket and keep me company while I'm sitting here" Preme said. Ant turned and ducked into his cell to retrieve his bucket. While Ant was in his cell, he heard Easy ask Preme: "What... my company ain't enough?" Ant remained in the cell, waiting to hear Preme's response before walking back out.

"Bitch please. I am paying you damn good money to do a service, so you just concentrate on that. Got it?" Ant came back out and placed his bucket in the doorway of his cell. Easy had begun to braid and no one was saying a word; it was Easy who broke the silence. "So, how many days you get for the fight Preme?"

"I got a little 15 days." Preme answered, trying to sound modest. "Damn! You came off. Everyone had figured that you'd get the max, but I guess since Magic signed himself into PC (which stands for Protective Custody), I guess they figured what the hell right? They won't be fighting anymore, so let's cut him a break." At the mention of PC, both Preme and Ant looked at each other and suddenly became interested with what Easy was saying. "How do you know Magic signed in?" Asked a curious Preme. Ant, sat on the edge of his bucket anxiously awaiting Easy's response.

"How do I know?" Easy repeated, as he held a portion of Preme's hair in one hand, and placing the other hand on his chest in a very dramatic flair. As Ant sat there watching and listening, he came to the conclusion that Easy was on the sweet side. Anyone else would have come to that realization immediately, or at least when Preme called Easy a bitch, but Ant wasn't like everyone else; he was extremely "green". Easy continued braiding and began doing what he obviously loved doing the most; and that was talking. "Everyone knows Magic signed in. Plus, you know I work with the pack-up officer, so I was the one who packed his cell up." Preme and Ant looked at each other again, and this time Preme asked Ant without uttering a word, if he wanted to hear more. Ant caught the look and nodded, letting Preme know he was okay with hearing whatever information Easy had. Right then, neither of them had time to contemplate on the fact that in such a short time, they could communicate without even opening their mouths.

"Alright Easy, give us the word that's out on the streets. And don't sugar-coat or withhold anything" demanded Preme.

"Are you sure you wanna hear all this, especially you Choir Boy... I mean Ant?" Easy asked, being just as theatrical as before. "Yeah, we sure. Ain't that right Ant?"

"That's correct, so spill it" stated Ant, who desperately wanted to add bitch to the end of his response, but thought better of it. Easy knew they was both thirsty for the goods, so he took his time, making them wait a bit. Preme knew the game Easy was playing and he let it be known. "Are you going to tell us, or do I have to beat it out of you?" Easy knew Preme was not one to be reckoned with, for he took no tea for the fever, as the old folks used to say; and decided to stop with the games. "Well, Magic told the popo that if he stayed in GP (General Population), you could have him done, because you have so much money and can buy just about anyone you so desire." This didn't come as a big surprise to Preme or Ant. But, Preme realized that he had to be very careful who he did business with from here on out. "Got that. What else?" Preme stated then questioned.

"Well, the rest of it is a bit more..." Easy stopped, as if searching for the right word. When he found it, his face showed it, and then he finished... "scandalous, let's just say."

"I'm not gonna tell you again, save the damn performance and just tell us the rest."

"Well, the word is that Choir Boy, that's what they call you Ant, is on the down low... you know, way back in the closet." Ant literally had to shake off anger. Like Preme had said after the fight with Magic, you can't control the thinking of others; especially the ignorant (he didn't say it in those exact words, but that was the jest of it). Easy continued with the gossip. "They are saying that Choir Boy was walking around here like he was too good to get with anybody until you came along Preme."

"What! You are joking right?" Preme asked, trying not to let his rage show.

"This is what they're saying Preme. They're saying that you are taking care of him across the board. You know, clothes, food, the whole nine and in return Choir Boy takes care of you." Neither Ant nor Preme responded, so Easy kept right on talking. "They said you took it personal when Magic stepped to you and questioned you about him. Magic wasn't under the impression that y'all was in such a serious relationship, he just thought y'all was having some fun and getting your rocks off. But ain't nobody really sweating you Preme; there are so many freaks walking around here, so they admire you the most for pulling the one they couldn't."

"First, it ain't that type of party. So, you can save all that and take it back to those fools out there talking." Preme sternly told Easy. "Preme, this isn't my view. I'm just telling you what's being spread. That's the reason I didn't want to say anything." Lied Easy, who was praying he was given an opportunity to address the mess.

"You're right, I asked you to tell me. But now I need you to do me a favor. GO back and tell those bitches to get their shit straight. I'll be out before they know it, and they don't want it with me." Easy just nodded as he completed the last braid. Preme produced a $20 bill from his sock and handed it to Easy. As Easy was about to leave, Preme asked him one more question: "Easy, was that everything that's being spread?" Easy stopped and thought for a minute; "Yeah, that's about it, other than the fags being upset that Choir Boy pulled you and they couldn't." With that, Easy gathered his things and headed toward the front of the gallery, where he would exit stage left. Preme and Ant watched him walk through the gate. Once he was gone, they looked at each other and shook their heads in disbelief. "Unbelievable." Ant stated.

"Unbelievable ain't even the word." With that, Preme picked up his bucket and stepped into the cell. No sooner than he crossed the threshold, the gate began to close. Ant continued to sit there with his mind in turmoil. For a few minutes, Ant was stuck in that spot. Had it not been for CO Simmons calling him, he probably would've been there for a much longer time. "Morgan, shift is about to change. Lock in until my relief gets here." Once in his cell, Ant sat on the bed, lost in his own jumbled thoughts.

****

It was just after 9pm, and Ant was sitting on the bed thinking. He knew the only way to find out more about Preme, was to first get his own story out the way. For some strange reason, ant knew there was something Preme was certainly with-holding, and he wanted to know what it was. Ant noticed how quiet the gallery was tonight, which was not the norm for this time of night; usually, TV's and radios were blasting as well as people yelling back and forth. From the reflection of the windows on the gallery, Ant could see Preme sitting on the bed, staring at the TV. Ant decided being that the gallery was so quiet, he'd see if Preme wanted to pull up on the gate early. Ant pulled up to his spot at the gate and tapped on the wall. Preme grabbed his mirror, came to the gate and put it between both cells so they could see each other.

"What up Ant?"

"Yo, I was figuring, being that it's so quiet, and I have been putting off telling you the rest of what happened. If you wanted, we could chop it up now that way I'll be able to finish it once and for all. What you think?" Ant questioned. Preme had been thinking the very same thing. For the moment, he had his issues in check and was once again ready to hear about the rest of Ant's life. "Yo, I'm cool with that; just give me a second to turn off this TV and get situated." Preme disappeared from the gate. Ant got up from his spot and went to the toilet to take a leak. Once that was completed, he returned his spot and awaited Preme's return, which came about 30 seconds later. Preme got comfortable and placed his arm out with the mirror. "I'm ready whenever you are" Preme said.

"Do you remember where I left off?" Ant inquired. "Yeah, I remember; you tried to end it, but thank God that wasn't successful."

"Right, well…"

****

Ant was rushed and treated at Bellevue Hospital in Manhattan. Bellevue is a full medical facility, but it's designed to treat the mentally ill. Crazy folks. After Ant was treated, he was kept in observation for 72 hrs. He wasn't even allowed any clothing whatsoever; they wouldn't even give him a blanket. At night it was so cold that Ant's teeth chattered non-stop. They even chattered when he was asleep. When the 72 hrs. were up, and the doctors determined that there was nothing mentally wrong with Ant, he was placed in a van along with two CO's in route back to the Rock.

As Ant sat in the van watching the sights of Manhattan, he thought about the three days, butt naked in that cold room, and decided that he would never attempt suicide again. He made this decision not so much because of the cold room, even though it did play a part. But because of the deep conviction that had set in. Ant knew that he grieved the Lord with his antics. Tears rolled down his cheeks as he silently asked for the Lord's forgiveness. It was clear that God kept him for a reason, and he vowed never to succumb to that demonic spirit of suicide again. Ant knew it wasn't going to be easy, but he would start and conclude every single day in prayer and the reading of God's word, a.k.a the B-I-B-L-E. Ant knew that was the only way he would overcome and defeat that demon. As the ride progressed, Ant sat back and an old hymn came to mind: "One day at a time, sweet Jesus. That's all I'm asking of you." That's exactly how he was going to have to face the future... One day at a time.

Ant had been back on the Rock for a week now. Upon his return, he was taken back to his old dorm; Mod 6. With the exception of two new faces, everybody was still there. When Ant had walked in, everyone became quiet and still; they all thought they were seeing a ghost. It was Culo who broke the silence. He ran to where Ant was standing, threw his arms around him, and broke down in tears. Ant was totally caught off guard by this, but still placed an arm around him, trying to console the boy. While doing so, the other guys in the dorm came around and began patting Ant on the shoulders, as well as expressing their joy that he was okay. Ant felt a sense of love and belonging. A feeling that he had not felt in a very long time. Ant didn't know how much longer he'd have this feeling of love and belonging with these individuals, because he would eventually have to go upstate to complete his time. However long he had with the Mod 6 crew, Ant decided to cherish it… He didn't know if he'd ever feel like this once he left.

Chapter 16

As Ant was being greeted by his Mod 6 buddies, Shadrack was driving out of the rental car parking lot at JFK airport. It was dark, but it was still too early for his meeting with Peaches. If he had taken a later flight, he would've been too late. The flight from Vegas had been long and uneventful, but Shadrack didn't mind that. He used the time to get his mind in tune with being back in New York again. After the business with Anthony, and after the members of Greater Second Chance Love Revival Tabernacle had up and left, Shadrack and Sylvia had discreetly sold their house and the church and re-located to Vegas. Money was not an issue, Shadrack and Sylvia had plenty of money in the bank. Then, after selling the house and church, they were more than just alright... they were rich.

Shadrack had chosen Vegas for two reasons: first, it was far away, and he was positive he could rebuild there without the fear of anyone knowing what happened in the Big Apple. The other reason was because he had a friend there who knew him and his fetish for young boys, and still remained a loyal friend. The reason for the loyalty was because this friend had a secret too; he also loved young boys and girls... and he too was a pastor. The Rev. Willie Laeitgood, who pastors "The Abundance of Love Devine Revelation Temple Church", who if given a few moments... could convince a whore to hang up her pleather stilettos and mini-skirt, while convincing a loving wife and mother to put them on and work the strip. It was not a surprise that Laeitgood's services were always packed.

Shadrack and Laeitgood were both from Florida. Different areas, but Florida none the less. They had seen each other several times, but never spoke. Shadrack had passed Laeitgood several times at an out of the way motel a few miles out of Pensacola. Laeitgood would be with his young flavor of the month, while Shadrack would take his nine-year-old stepson for a little "recreation". No matter how hard Shadrack tried not to be seen, it seemed that he and Laeitgood (whose name he did not know at the time) always managed to run into one another.

When Shadrack had married his first wife Christine, her sone Jermaine, who they called Baby J, was only four-years-old. Shadrack had waited until he was six before he began to have his way with him. Christine wasn't nowhere near as outgoing and occupied as his present wife Sylvia. All Christine did when she wasn't at church,was cook, clean, and watch TV all day & night. She was so unpredictable, that's why Shadrack was forced to always take Baby J outside of the house for some "fun".

Shadrack had no idea who Laeitgood was or that he was a preacher until about a year after... Shadrack ran into him at a service in Tampa. Shadrack had been invited to an appreciation service for an old high school buddy, who opened a church in Tampa. It happened that this buddy's wife had a cousin who was also a preacher. He was called on at the service to do the opening prayer; the Rev. Willie Laeitgood. When Laeitgood came to the podium, Shadrack almost fell out of his chair, and his name... forget about it. After service, Shadrack and Laeitgood talked for a while, and vowed to never rat on one another. They became the best of friends. They had even fallen into bed together a few times, but their real love was for the young and innocent. When Laeitgood had been run out of Florida for impregnating and 11-year-old congregant, Shadrack had been a supportive friend. Now, the shoe was on the other foot, and Laeitgood was returning the favor.

ChoirBoy

****

Shadrack still had plenty of time before his meeting at the motel. He decided to drive pass the old house and building that had once been his church. Shadrack drove quickly and just glanced at the building; he had a new life now, and he didn't want to be bombarded with thoughts of the old life and the "what if's". As he drove with no destination in mind or urgency, there was one place he couldn't keep his mind from going; Anthony. There was no doubt in his mind that the boy was someone's bitch behind bars; he was just too damn soft.

With an hour away before his meeting, Shadrack decided to head in the direction of the motel, but he'd take the backstreets instead of the expressway. Thinking about Anthony always brought mixed feelings. He really loved the boy (if you call that love) and had such high hopes for him. Had the boy been a bit cooperative, Shadrack had contemplated cutting off all his other sexual involvements. He would have been content between Sylvia and Anthony's beds! But no, the boy had to go and screw everything up! Now, Shadrack had to start all over and build his new church from the ground up. He was already making a name for himself, thanks to Laeitgood, who had him preaching at his church on a regular basis, as well as introducing him to all the key pastors in Vegas and the surrounding areas. The plan was for Shadrack to open a "sister" church to Laeitgood's about an hour away. That way, Shadrack would get all the members Laeitgood would have gotten, had it not been too far and time consuming to get to. Shadrack had decided to name the new church The Greater Love Without Limits Devine Revelation Temple Church.

As a red light forced Shadrack to stop, he pushed Vegas out of his mind and thought of Anthony again. There was no doubt in his mind that they would see each other again, but hopefully by then, the boy will have come to his senses and it would be a joyous reunion. Upon the light turning green, Shadrack slowly pulled off, and this time his mind went to his wife Sylvia, who was back in Vegas. Shadrack had no idea what a cold hearted and materialistic bitch Sylvia was when he married her. Now, don't get it twisted, he was grateful that he has what it takes to control her and keep her loyalty. What surprised Shadrack was the fact that she would disown her own son to remain in his bed and sport Dolce & Gabbana. There was no doubt in his mind that Sylvia would murder someone if Shadrack told her to. Especially if it threatened their lifestyle. Shadrack realized that he had gotten more than what he bargained for when it came to Sylvia.

Shadrack hadn't realized until now, driving through the borough of Queens, how much he missed New York. Not that he disliked Vegas, but there was always something very special about the Big Apple… the city that never sleeps. Yes, he missed it, but he had to count his blessings. The situation here in NY could have been much worse, but he came out with nothing more than a few scrapes and bruises. Looking back in retrospect, he always came out like that. Then he thought back to Florida, and Baby J's suicide. Had the truth come out, Shadrack knew more than likely he'd be dead right now. He often thought about Christine and the child that she was about to give birth to. If Christine did know the truth, she chose never to reveal it and moved on. It never once crossed Shadrack's mind to slow down and just fall back. In his mind, he really believed that he'd always come out smelling like a rose.

ChoirBoy

Shadrack looked at his watch, and realized he had wasted enough time. He should have been walking into the room, right this very moment. He quickly pulled off the main streets and headed towards the expressway. Within six minutes from getting on the expressway, he was now sitting at a red light, a mere two blocks from the motel. As he sat there, his mind raced back to the last time he was at the motel. Peaches had brought a friend by the name of Precious, and what a time they had. Shadrack's body began to grow warm from anticipation of what possibilities and surprises awaited him tonight. The streets were deserted as Shadrack drove the last few feet to the motel. Like before, he parked directly in front of the room and made a mad dash from the car to the unlocked room. Once inside, before doing anything, Shadrack locked the door and made sure that it was secure. Once that was done, he turned to survey the room. There sitting on the bed, nursing a drink that looked and smelled like a Long Island Iced Tea, was Peaches… looking ripe and pure in a skin tight purple suede suit. Shadrack could tell that it was tight. Just by the way he was sitting, with his leg crossed, showing the perfect thigh compressed in the soft, tight material. "Are we alone?" asked Shadrack.

"Of course we're alone. Who else did you expect… Santa Claus?" responded Peaches, being true to his form, giving Shadrack his trade-mark attitude. "Well, last time we were here, you had a friend Precious with you" said a somewhat disappointed Shadrack, secretly hoping there would be a surprise waiting. Shadrack hoped that his voice response did not reveal his disappointment. He and Peaches always had a good time together, with or without Precious.

"Well, that was last time. Since then, I discovered that I come off a lot better working on my own; I can't afford to

split any more money. If you're disappointed that it's just
you and me, I can take my merchandise and go elsewhere.
"Oh no, I'm glad that it's just you and me tonight. It's been
sometime since just you and I did business" responded
Shadrack, revealing how very thirsty and desperate he
was.

 "Alright then, let's get down to business" stated Peaches,
who at the same time pointed to a corner in the room
where at least ten huge shopping bags were filled with
boosted goods. Peaches continued talking, "all the men's
gear is in your size, being that you're no longer shopping
for your step-son these days." "You got that right"
Shadrack said sarcastically. "And of course, all the female
gear is in Mrs. Brown's size. But, before you go looking at
the goodies I lifted, and before we began discussing
prices… let's have a drink." Peaches hated playing nice to
this scumbag, but to get what he needed tonight, he had to
be nice. If this went down correctly, Peaches wouldn't
have to boost again. He'd be able to shop where he
wanted, and do so with nothing but cash. Plus, Peaches
had his eye on a cute pearl white Lexus Coupe. Peaches
knew he had to work this just right.

 Peaches got up from the bed and sashayed across the
room to the small table, where he placed the bottles and
glasses. Peaches poured Shadrack a tall glass of the spirit,
and brought it to Shadrack who was now sitting on the
edge of the bed. Shadrack took the glass and took a sip.
"No, no, no Rev., this is a celebration that you're back in
the Big Apple . We don't sip the first one, we take it straight
to the head." "And how does one take it to the head my
dear Peaches?" asked Shadrack, clearly thinking it had a
hidden sexual meaning. Peaches wanted to gag at
Shadrack's triflin' ass, but he thought about the Lexus, and
answered accordingly.

"It means you drink the entire glass in one swallow. You haven't forgotten how to swallow, have you Rev?" Peaches asked teasingly, playing the role. "That is one thing I could never forget, for there are so many wonderful things to swallow." "Well, here's to us." They clicked glasses and the both tilted their heads back, gulping the liquid until it was gone. Peaches quickly refilled Shadrack's glass. "Rev., you sit there and sip on your drink and I'll show you what I lifted for you." Shadrack sipped on his drink as Peaches went to the shopping bags over in the corner. Shadrack didn't think he ever had one of these Long Island Iced Teas, but it sure was good. It was so good that he finished off the second glass, got up and poured himself some more. Once that was accomplished, he sat down on the bed and was already beginning to feel nice.

Over the next hour Peaches slowly took out each and every item and showed Shadrack, giving him designer names and prices. In between, Peaches made sure Shadrack's glass was never empty. When the show and tell was completed, Peaches could tell Shadrack was good and tipsy because he was extremely talkative and animated. Peaches could also tell that the Rev's attention was close to non-existent. Peaches walked over to the little desk in front of the bed and pressed the record button on the camcorder that was concealed in a leather hand bag. There was a hole in the bag that would allow the recorder to record everything on the bed. Peaches came and sat down next to Shadrack, who immediately placed his hand on Peaches leg and began to rub it. Peaches politely moved his hand and spoke. "Rev., we'll have plenty of time for that. Being that it's been such a long time since we've seen each other, I figured it would be nice to talk for a little while and get caught up."

"We can talk while we're doing the nasty" Shadrack said as he tried to grab Peaches, who was too fast for him, and stopped him before he made contact. What Peaches really wanted to do was kill the sick bastard, but again thought of the rewards for putting up with Shadrack's pedophile ass. "Shadrack, if we don't talk, there won't be any fun and games tonight. Trust!"

"Oh, alright! Let's talk." Shadrack replied with a sulk on his face, still sitting on the edge of the bed next to Peaches. "So, where are you living these days Rev?" Shadrack began to chuckle, waving his index finger as if telling a child no and he replied: "Oh no, you know I can't tell you that. No sir, can't tell ya."

"Shadrack, you mean to tell me after all the stuff we've shared through the years, you act as if you can't trust me. You know what? I'm outta here." Peaches jumped up from the bed as if he was really going to leave, and grabbed his suede jacket that was resting on the chair nearby. Even in Shadrack's drunken stupor, he was alert enough to know he didn't want Peaches to leave. "No Peaches, come back and sit down; I'll tell you, IF… you promise to keep it a secret." Peaches didn't realize until that moment just how sprung Shadrack was. Sure, her knew Shadrack was a freak, and liked them young, but Shadrack needed sex like he needed the air he breathed. Peaches placed his jacket back on the chair and with a reluctant like performance, he sat back down on the bed.

"No more secrets Rev.?" Peaches asked

"No more secrets Peaches, I promise" responded Shadrack, as if he was a five-year-old that just got reprimanded.

"So where are you and the Mrs. Living?"

"Cross your heart you won't tell?" Shadrack asked in a voice that was straight up whiny.

"You know Shadrack..." Peaches was about to blast his fat ass, but caught himself and answered sweetly, "Yes, I cross my heart." Peaches crossed his heart and moved closer to Shadrack, but not close enough that they were touching. In an instant Shadrack transformed. A smile came across his face and he bellowed his response.

"We're in the 702 baby! You know, Las Vegas, Nevada! Where there's stacks of chips and dream house money." It was obvious that Shadrack had watched one too many rap videos on BET. "What made you decide to move to Vegas? You know people there?" Peaches questioned, excited that he was finally getting somewhere with this jerk off.

"I only know one person there, but I'm about to open a new church there." Shadrack stated, who's tongue was now loose, thanks to the Long Island Iced Tea.

"Is that right? Who's this friend and what does he do?"

"He's a pastor, and his church's name is Abundance of Love Devine Revelation Temple Church, and I'm opening a sister church about an hour drive away. The name of my church will be The Greater Love Without Limits Devine Revelation Temple Church." Shadrack finally stopped talking, but the mouse that ate the cheese grin remained.

"Oh, so what's the Pastor's name?"

"The Rev. Willie Laeitgood." Shadrack stated as a matter of fact. Peaches on the other hand, thought he heard something wrong.

"What did you say his name is?"

"It's true; his name is Willie Laeitgood." Shadrack leaned over and whispered "And he likes both young boys and girls." Peaches had to fight his sudden urge to puke, he couldn't believe this nasty shit. The Lexus coupe flashed across his mind and he got a grip. "You sure that's his real name?" Peaches asked, still not believing it.

"Just as sure as my name is Shadrack E. Brown, and the "E" stands for erect." With that, Shadrack burst out laughing. Peaches on the other hand was repulsed to the ninth degree, but realized there was still a lot more information that he needed to acquire. And there was no telling what the information might entail.

"Willie Laeitgood." Peaches repeated still not believing. "He's alright, but not as good as he says he is though" Shadrack stated. This shit was more than unbelievable thought Peaches. It was Hollywood, and just like MGM and Paramount made tons of money, Peaches planned to do the same. "How do you know this Willie Laeitgood? Peaches asked. "I know him from Florida, but he got an 11-year-old girl pregnant and had to get the hell outta dodge. Next thing I knew, he was in the 702." As bad as Peaches wanted to remain on this topic, he knew he had to move on and get the information concerning Anthony.

"Shadrack, what happened between you and Anthony?" "He shot me! That light eyed bitch shot me right here" Shadrack pulled up his shirt and pointed to his wound. Peaches and the entire Tri-State area knew Anthony had shot him. What they didn't know was why. Peaches also knew that he was treading on dangerous grounds asking these questions. To be sure that the conversation would continue to go smoothly, Peaches got up and poured Shadrack a half a glass of the tea. He handed it to Shadrack, who downed the alcohol as if was just a sip.

Peaches sat back down and started probing again. "Yeah, that was bad that he shot you."

"You damn right it was bad" Shadrack interrupted and stated indignantly.

"Especially after all you did for him. I know first-hand you kept him in the latest and hottest gear, thanks to me."

"Yup, I sure did… I sure did."

"So, why did he shoot you?" Peaches asked.

"The brazen little bastard said he was tired of me taking his ass, but I know he wanted it, even though he wouldn't admit it."

"How long had you been having him?" Peaches used the word "having" even though he knew he had been taking the boy.

"Oh, I waited until he was older before I climbed on him; he was six or seven."

Peaches gagged, but knew this was the information he was being paid to get on tape, so he pressed on sounding intrigued. "So, you went into little Anthony's room that night for some fun and he shot you instead huh?"

"That's what happened. Yes, that's exactly what happened" said Shadrack, slurring each word.

"Mm. Does Mrs. Brown know what was going on?" Peaches wanted to hear this answer, because that would let him in on the mind of Sylvia, who wanted her son to do the maximum time in prison.

"She knows, but she loves me more than she loves him. Plus, I take good care of that bitch."

Peaches couldn't fathom the fact that Sylvia turned he back on her own flesh and blood for this scumbag. Now, he was starting to see the reason this information would be so valuable, if used properly. "So, neither you or the Mrs. have anything to do with Anthony I take it."

"That's right, he no longer belongs to us anymore. I'm sure he's someone's bitch by now, up in the big house.

Peaches listened to Shadrack and determined whatever his employer (the person paying for all this information) had in store for Shadrack, more than likely wouldn't measure up to what this bastard really deserves. Peaches knew he had to keep digging. "You were married before Sylvia right Rev.?"

"Sure was. When I was back in Florida, but the bitch ran off and left me."

"What's her name?"

"Christine. Christine the cunt" answered Shadrack.

Peaches now understood what the old folks meant when they said that alcohol was a truth serum. "Did the two of you have any children?"

"She had Baby J, my favorite boy of all time." Shadrack stated with dreamy eyes and continued. "And she was pregnant when I asked her to marry me, but it wasn't my baby and I knew it from the start, but that was okay."

"You sure it wasn't your baby Rev.?"

"Hell yeah I'm sure. I needed a family, so I bought one. In my profession, appearance is everything. A family made me look complete and wholesome. That's wholesome."

"You and Baby J were very close I take it?"

"Oh, how I loved that boy. I couldn't keep my hands off of him." Peaches could tell that Shadrack's mind was in reminiscing mode.

"Have you ever tried to find Baby J?"

"Baby J is gone."

"Yeah, I know, but have you ever tried to find him?" asked Peaches.

"Baby J is gone forever. He killed himself." Shadrack stated, as a tear rolled down his cheek. Peaches needed to move on, despite the fact that his own curiosity kicked in. He really wanted to know how Baby J died, and the rest of the details involving that, but he couldn't chance that Shadrack would continue to hold up and tell all like he had been doing. "Did Christine have the second baby?"

"I guess she did, but she ran out on me four weeks before she was due."

"So, you don't even know if she had a boy or a girl. Or if she even had the baby?"

"That's right, I don't."

"I mean, why do you think Christine just up and left you?"

Shadrack sat on the bed, as tears began to pour from his eyes. Peaches knew this conversation was just about over. "She left me, because I'm the reason Baby J took his life. She never said anything, but I could tell when I looked at her, that she knew." Shadrack's voice began to break, and the tears fell in a rapid concession. He laid back on the bed and Peaches could tell that the alcohol would have him sleep in moments, so he posed one last question.

"Rev., you're saying, you're the reason Baby J died, as well as Anthony being in prison?" Peaches held his breath waiting for Shadrack's response.

With a tear stained face, Shadrack replied; "Yes! It was all because of me!" Shadrack began to sob uncontrollably as Peaches sat there and just watched him, trying to absorb all the information he had just learned. Peaches didn't know how long he had sat in that spot, but when he finally came to himself, Shadrack was snoring. Peaches got up and collected his things, as well as money from Shadrack's wallet to cover the cost of the merchandise. When all was gathered, Peaches grabbed the bag that held the camcorder, turned the machine off and headed for the door. When Peaches had the door open, before he stepped out, he turned and just looked at Shadrack. Pure disgust plagued him. Peaches remembered his jacket and quickly retrieved it from the chair and left the room, closing the door behind him. Peaches made up in his mind on the way to his ride, that this would be the very last time he would be that close to Shadrack E. Brown again! He didn't care how much money was being offered. But then again, if the price was right... and he meant RIGHT, he might have to reconsider.

Chapter 17

Peaches got to his ride, and without hesitation, got up out of the area with the quickness. After driving for about five minutes, he pulled over on the side of the road and pulled his cell phone from his leather bag. The same one that held the camcorder. Peaches dialed a number, and after ten rings, the man answered. "Yeah?" the voice on the line asked.

"I got what you asked for."

"You got all of it?" The voice on the line asked.

"I got what you asked for, and then some. There's something real juicy on here that will bring earnings of at least double what we originally agreed on." Peaches held his breath, hoping he wasn't playing himself with this dude. The last thing Peaches needed was drama; he'd have enough of that once he got back to Brooklyn.

"I'll have to see this information that you're bragging about. Meet me at the spot in an hour". With that, the stranger hung up the phone. Peaches replaced the phone, got the car in motion and headed for Harlem.

****

Two hours and twenty minutes later, Peaches was sitting in an office with his employer. They had just reviewed the video Peaches took a few hours ago. Peaches was tired and ready to go home and crawl into bed. The sun would be out in another 45 minutes, and Peaches wanted to be back in Brooklyn by then, or close to it. Peaches employer sat there for a few minutes and stared at the screen. Peaches didn't want to know how long he could sit there like that, so, he posed a question in hopes that it would break him out of his trance. "Are you pleased with all the additional information that I got you?"

The employer looked at Peaches, and then got up from his chair. He went to a file cabinet that sat on the back wall of the office. He opened the top drawer and removed a large, stuffed, manilla envelope. "Yes, I am Peaches; you did good." He walked back to his spot and handed Peaches the envelope. Peaches took the envelope, but did not open it, despite his urge to. "There is $50,000 in there. Double what I agreed to give you. You were right. Some of that info is worth $50,000 alone, but a deal is a deal." Peaches got up, grabbed his jacket and was about to leave when his employer spoke again: "Peaches, I appreciate your hard work. But I won't be needing you again. At least not for this."

"That's good, because I have no desire to ever see him again."

"You were well paid, so I can assume this business stays between us, right?""Yes, you can rest assure. But I do have on question: Why is this guy so important to you?" Peaches knew he was "pushing the envelope" so to speak, by asking this question, but what the hell? Scared money don't make no money; right?

"That my friend is T.M.I. Get home safe, and don't spend all that money in one place. And with that, Peaches nodded and walked out the back door that led to the alley where his car was parked. Once Peaches was gone, the man sat down and held the video tape he had just purchased. Things were coming together, slowly but surely, he thought. He was in no rush, and was willing to wait however long it took.

****

ChoirBoy

Three hours after Peaches had left the motel, a drunken Shadrack, laid out on the bed snoring, was awakened by the constant ringing of the telephone. When Shadrack opened his eyes, day light caused his head to pound all the more. The phone continued to ring, and with slow efforts that brought him pain with every move, Shadrack answered the phone. "Yeah, yeah, what is it?" an angry and hung over Shadrack barked into the phone.

"Sir, your time is up on the room. If you desire additional time, we'll need the payment upfront" the female clerked stated, hating this part of her job the most.

"What time is it?" Shadrack questioned, coming to his senses.

"Sir, it's 5:30 am." Shadrack's flight back to Vegas wasn't due to depart until 9:30, meaning he had at least three hours to rest and get himself together.

"Yeah, give me three more hours on the room, and give me a wakeup call at 8:00."

"We will need the money in advance sir. Three hours will cost $45.00. Will that be alright with you?"

"Yeah, send someone over to get it; I'll slide the money under the door." With that, Shadrack slammed the phone down. He laid back down and thought about the previous night. There wasn't much he remembered. He did remember Peaches being in the room when he got there, and that Peaches was showing him all the items he boosted. He did recall having a drink or two, but not enough to make him feel like this. He looked over to a corner of the room, and saw the bags with his purchases sitting there. Shadrack quickly rolled off the bed to grab his wallet from the little eating table. Each step hurt like hell, but he managed to get there. He quickly opened his wallet. His credit cards, identification and money were still there, minus the money for the items in the corner. Shadrack walked back to the bed again and laid back down.

"Why the hell did he leave?" Shadrack asked out loud to an empty room. Shadrack remembered that he was never good at holding his liquor. He wondered if he revealed anything that he shouldn't have, like where he was living. There were still people out there like Harold, and God know who else, that wanted to get their hands on him. He then remembered that Peaches went into his wallet, so it was a very good possibility that he knew where he was living. Peaches wouldn't tell anyone, he thought to himself. If he had not told on him after all these years, why would he start now? Well, there was nothing he could do about it now, and it sure didn't make sense to sit here and dwell on it. What he couldn't understand, was why he left without giving him a fix. These meetings were about the tune up, more so than the clothes. Shadrack decided to give himself a quick fix, in hopes that he would feel better. He slowly pulled his pants down as his mind swarmed with images of young male flesh.

****

Six hours later Shadrack was sitting in his first-class seat by the window, heading home. He was feeling a lot better thanks to an entire pot of black coffee, and eight extra strength Tylenols. Shadrack's mind went to his new life he was building in Vegas. He knew he had to make some changes so that he wouldn't have to go through what he shamefully endured in New York, as well as Florida. Right then and there, he made up in his mind to never do business with Peaches again. Sure, he enjoyed their encounters. But he couldn't chance it with him anymore, especially after deserting him in the motel like he did. Shadrack had plenty of money, so there was no reason he would need to keep purchasing boosted goods from a flaming fag who was on his way to hell in a handbasket. No more would he cut corners. From now on, he would live life to the fullest. Shadrack had no idea why he was suddenly feeling like this. But he wondered, if the opportunity presented itself again, would he remain steadfast... probably not. But for now, that was his stand. Shadrack sat back and closed his eyes, anxious to get back to Las Vegas.

****

Three weeks after Ant had returned to the Rock from the hospital, he was awakened at 3:30 in the morning and was told by the CO that he was being transferred Upstate. Ant knew this day was coming, but now that it was here, he wasn't ready for it. Ant got up, took care of his hygiene, and began to pack his belongings. He had heard so many terror stories about prisons Upstate that he couldn't help but be scared. He was almost positive that he wouldn't know anybody, and that had its advantages as well as it's disadvantages. The advantage was he could be left alone, and wouldn't have people divulging into his life. However, on the other hand, he would be extremely lonely and that's the thing Ant struggled with the most; loneliness.

The thing that Ant couldn't understand was, after all the hurt, abuse, betrayal and injustices he had been through, how could he still have so much love in his heart. Ant was one of those individuals who was always sensitive to others feelings and situations. For instance, Ant could see an old man shopping in Western Beef (when he used to work there) who seemed so alone in the world, and Ant would run to the bathroom to hide his tears. To Ant, having these feelings despite what he went through, was an oxymoron. Now, on his way Upstate, he knew he would have to keep his emotions in check and stay to himself. That way, he'd remain safe. Both physically and emotionally.

Ant began getting his belongings together, lost in thought. He was totally oblivious to the fact that Culo had woken up and was making his way over to him. Ant noticed, that for such a young man, Culo looked really ragged and worn… well beyond his years. "Don't tell me they're packing you up Ant." Culo stated, after having reached Ant's side. Culo's breath was hot and rancid; Ant hoped it was due to the fact that he had just woken up.

"Yeah, I'm on my way Upstate to do this time." Ant replied, while still packing his things into a large plastic garbage bag. For the next few moments, neither one spoke, but both having things that they wanted to say to one another… finally, Ant broke the silence. "Culo, I never said thank you for saving my life. There are people who would have went on with their business, and wouldn't have gotten help. I appreciate what you did, and I'll never forget it." Ant stopped talking, because his emotions were on the verge of going hay wire.

"Ant, you be careful when you get Upstate. I already know that you've been through a lot. But God brought you through it, and he will always do so. No matter what the situation is, there's no excuse for you to take your life." Culo's voice began to crack. He took a few deep breaths then continued: "Ant, that night when you saw me in the stall with my daddy, I saw the way you looked and how intrigued you were." Ant opened his mouth to deny it, but Culo silenced him and proceeded to make his point. "Just listen. I know what you've been through, because I've been through it too." Ant did a double take, and dropped his jaw in unbelief. "My uncle had started taking me when I was ten, and that's all I've ever known. There is no other hope for me Ant; this is the only life I know. You, on the other hand, are one of the fortunate ones. No matter how rough it gets, promise me you won't get involved in this madness. Trust what I tell you."

Ant was shocked and embarrassed that Culo was able to read him so very accurately. But there was more to it. Ant knew what it was he was feeling, and that was the presence of the Lord. He knew God was speaking to him. Many would say that God wouldn't use a practicing homosexual, but if God could use a jackass, he could use anyone (not that he would consistently use a homo, unless he got saved, but for a purpose as such, it was known to happen). There was no doubt in his mind that God was speaking through Culo. "Ant, what you've been through doesn't have to keep you bound forever... the choice is yours. Promise me that you'll choose correctly, and you won't ever get involved in this life. Promise me!"

Ant was glad everyone was asleep, because a tear had fell and if he didn't get himself under control, he would've broken down in tears. Culo took Ant's hand and sternly whispered; "Promise me Ant." Ant took his free hand, wiped his eye and said "I promise." Without any thoughts of insecurity or being ashamed, Ant pulled Culo into an embrace. They patted each other on the back like two homeboys, and when they parted, tears were on both their cheeks.

"Give me your Bible" Culo said to Ant. Ant turned and grabbed his bible off the bed, where he had left it so he could pack it last, and handed it to Culo. Culo took the Bible, opened it to the last page, took a pen from the top of

Ant's locker and began to write. When he finished writing, he gave the Bible back to Ant and began talking again. "I will be home in 77 days. When I get home, there better be a letter from you. If I have to track you down, you won't like me." Culo said in a playful yet serious tone. "Also, when you write, let me know if you need anything. I'll send it to you. Okay?" Ant didn't know what to say. He just nodded his head, letting Culo know he would do as stated.

"Alright, finish getting your stuff together. I'll go wake these heifers and let them know you're leaving; they'd kick my faggot ass if you had left and I didn't wake them up." Again, Ant nodded his head and Culo was off waking up everyone in Mod 6. 45 mins later, after having said his good-byes to his Mod 6 family, Ant walked out the dorm, uncertain of what awaited him. One thing he knew was that if it came his way, it meant that he could handle and survive it. Yes, Ant was nervous, but somewhere deep inside, he knew he'd make it.

Chapter 18

Ant ended up in an adolescent maximum-security jail, in a rural part of New York… about an hour drive from New York City. It wasn't an easy transition going from the Rock to an upstate facility. Especially an adolescent one. Yeah, there was constant drama on the Rock, especially in C-74. But this was another level entirely. When cells opened for breakfast at 7 am, within seconds, at least five separate fights would breakout throughout the facility. Whenever you heard "Red Dot" being yelled from the CO's walkie talkie, you knew it was on and poppin somewhere. The gym and the yards were war zones every time they were opened. In the first week of Ant's arrival, he had witnessed a cutting, a stabbing, and a murder. Ant was determined to stay clear of everyone and everything. Two weeks after his arrival, Ant was sent to the Program Committee where a daily work, school or vocational program is assigned to every inmate. Ant was given school, which he was glad, because he wanted to learn as much as possible.

When Ant wasn't in school, he was in his cell doing something constructive, like reading, writing or studying. This routine might have aggravated some, but it was just fine for Ant. There were 40 cells on the gallery in which Ant was housed. Everyone on the gallery accepted the fact that Ant was a loner. They would all greet him and vice versa, when they passed him. However, it was obvious that Ant wasn't looking to make friends. Showers were given every other evening on the gallery, but if you didn't go to the late afternoon recreation period, the gallery officer would allow whoever stayed in the chance to take their showers early. Ant, was still uneasy around other men, especially in this environment. He quickly found out that the entire gallery always went to the late afternoon recreation. This was great for him, because Ant didn't think he'd ever get used to showering with five other men.

One afternoon Ant was sitting on his bed with his towel wrapped around his waist, slippers on, soap and wash cloth in his hands, waiting for his cell to open so he could take his shower. Ant had been quietly singing an old Clark Sister's tune called "Is My Living in Vain" when his cell finally opened. Ant's cell was only three cells away from the shower area. He discarded the towel that had been tied tightly around his waist, and stepped into the hot flowing water. Ant closed his eyes, and began allowing the water to soothe him. As he began running the soap across his body, he began reminiscing about all the young girls he had slept with. With those thoughts and images in his head it was only normal that he would become aroused and indulge in his favorite past-time, which involved rosy palm and her five friends. Ant had gotten into the rhythm and was so engrossed, that he was unaware that Tiny had entered the shower. Tiny was 20 years-old, 6'8", 'bout 245 lb. convicted murder, who had been locked up since the age of 12. Tiny was quiet and all he did was eat and workout with the weights. Tiny hardly ever spoke to anyone, and because of his size… he was greatly feared.

Tiny had entered the shower, removed his green bathrobe and proceeded butt naked into the shower directly in front of Ant. Tiny was aware that Ant was in the shower in front of him, and at first, he was unaware of what he was doing. It wasn't until Ant began to moan, that Tiny realized what Ant was doing. Being that Tiny was so big and quiet, it wasn't known that he preferred boys over girls any day. Tiny wasn't thirsty in the sense that he went after every male that tickled his fancy; he was just the opposite. He was so fearful of being found out, that he was content with his imagination unless he knew it was a sure thing. Tiny had noticed Ant the minute he had arrived at this facility, and was immediately turned on by him. But like always, he kept it to himself, and alone in his cell at night he allowed his imagination, picturing what it would be like to be with Ant, to bring him pleasure.

Standing there watching Ant please himself, to Tiny, was an invitation. Tiny knew they were the only ones on the gallery. Plus, he knew the CO's were at their stations acting like the hicks they were, and would never walk down the gallery unless they had to. It couldn't have been more perfect. Tiny was dizzy with anticipation and longing, that it wasn't funny. When he could no longer stand it, Tiny walked over to where Ant was standing, still stroking himself, with his eyes closed… Tiny got down on his knees, with his face in line with Ant's penis. At first, Tiny just sat there staring, admiring Ant's beauty. Finally, Tiny opened his mouth and at the same time lifting his hand to Ant's penis, to guide it into his mouth. When Tiny made contact with Ant's flesh, Ant released a yell and pulled away, backing into the wall of the shower extremely hard. Tiny was too excited to realize that he made a mistake, but as he sat there stroking himself with one hand, he took the other and reached out to touch Ant again, but it all became very clear. Ant quickly went from being aroused, to furious & sickened. In Ant's mind. It wasn't Tiny on his knees before him, It was Shadrack. Ant quickly reacted and began punching and kicking Tiny anywhere the blows landed, all while giving him a verbal beating.

"You big dumb cock sucking faggot! How dare you put your nasty ass hands on me, you overgrown freak!" Ant continued to pounce on Tiny, who tried to block the blows and began begging for mercy.

"Please stop! I'm sorry." Tiny pleaded. Tiny sounded more like a young punk, than a big oversized beast. "I'm sorry man, please don't hit me no more." Tiny fell to the floor on his side and sobbed. Ant stopped for a moment and just looked down at Tiny in pure disgust. As angry as Ant was, he couldn't believe this big bitch was laying on the floor crying like a street whore, who just took a beating from her pimp. Ant stepped around the weeping heap on the floor, grabbed his towel and proceeded to put it back around his waist. Once that was accomplished, he gathered his belongings and was about to leave the area, when Tiny called out to him. "Ant please listen one minute." Tiny begged in between sobs. Something about the way Tiny spoke forced Ant to stop in his tracks, but he wouldn't turn around and look at him.

"I honestly thought you knew I was in here, and was doing that as you know... an invite. I'm sorry I violated you man, I swear I am." Tiny sobbed again and took a few seconds to regain his composure, while Ant remained silent. "Please don't say anything to anyone about this, please." There was such desperation in Tiny's voice, and what Ant detected to be sincerity. "I'll pay you if that's what it will take." Ant turned to see Tiny now sitting on the floor, with his head hung low. Ant just shook his head and walked back to his cell.

****

Twenty-one months from the day of the incident with Tiny, Ant was shackled hand and foot on a bus, headed to another facility. Ant sat there staring out of the window, thinking about the all the different things that took place at the facility he had just left. He recalled how afraid he was the first day he was there. How he was intimidated by the building size and construction. Then seeing the inmates with their angry glares, the constant battles and wars that transpired all day every day. Then he thought back to the situation that day in the shower with Tiny. A slight smile escaped him, as he remembered how Tiny begged, cried and pleaded for mercy. Remembering the situation with Tiny, Ant recalled the "new" Tiny that emerged following their encounter.

One day while Tiny was picking up his commissary from the store, he insisted that Ant take majority of it. Ant had tried desperately to refuse, but once Tiny made up his mind about something ,there was no changing it. Tiny even went as far as to have his family send Ant packages every month. The ultimate was, Tiny had become Ant's personal bodyguard and soldier. If someone looked like they had an issue with Ant, Tiny had no problem opening a can of whoop ass on them. One time, an entire gallery was in the commissary getting their bi-weekly groceries, and Ant was at the window shopping heavy this particular week. As Ant's purchases was went through the window, the items that were canned he would drop into his bag, and the items that could be squashed or broken, he placed on the ledge to his right and turned his attention back to the items coming through the window. There was a real slickster on the gallery named Bolo. Bolo was a blood and was notorious for cutting people faster than one could blink their eyes. He was a bully, and even most of the CO's were afraid of him. While Ant was at the window getting his groceries, Bolo was over on the side with three of his homies, and Tiny was standing far off in the back... alone. While Ant was talking to the civilian woman behind the window, Bolo creeped up and slipped two packs of chocolate chip soft batch cookies off the ledge, and slipped back over to his crew. Tiny didn't say a word, he just walked over to Bolo and commenced to beat him, just as Ant had done him in the shower that day.

"You punk bitch. Didn't your momma ever teach you not to touch stuff that doesn't belong to you?" By this time, everyone was watching the show. Ant was still up at the window, with no idea as to why Tiny was beating the boy. There was a CO present, but because Bolo was such a creep, he just sat there and refused to call for help. "Why don't you steal from me, you faggot?" Inwardly Ant laughed at that one, but didn't say anything. Bolo was bleeding from his nose and mouth, and pain racked his entire body. Bolo's homies felt bad for him, but they were not about to jump in.

"Enough!" Yelled the CO. He really didn't care if Tiny killed the sorry bastard, but he would get in trouble and lose his job; he had five kids, a wife and two dogs to feed. When Tiny heard the officer yell, he obediently ceased physically abusing Bolo, stepped back and placed his hands in the air. "Get up and give it back." Tiny demanded to the hurting and moaning heap curled up on the floor. By this time, Ant had finished at the window and was placing his belongings that were on the ledge in his bags, while keeping an eye on the action. "I ain't gonna tell you again." Tiny warned. Knowing he didn't want another beat down, Bolo pushed himself up off the floor and made his way over to where him and his homies had been chilling. Bolo went inside his $6.50 bag of groceries and produced the two packs of soft batch cookies. He painfully walked over to Ant, handed him the two packs of cookies, and turned and headed for the CO. Ant, on the other hand, stood there looking at the cookies he was now holding. He looked down at his bags and realized the cookies weren't in there; Bolo had sneakily thieved his damn cookies. What was even more astonishing, was the fact that Tiny had handled the situation without a word. Ant still had a hard time forgetting what Tiny had done that day in the shower, but Ant had accepted the role he played in that incident as well. Ant now held all his pleasure-capades in the confines of his cell, with the sheet up over the bars.

Three officers entered the commissary, one had a brief word with Bolo, who nodded his head to whatever the CO had asked him. He then went and grabbed his bag and he and the CO left. The other two talked with Tiny and then Tiny left with the officers in tow. Bolo never came back to that unit after the incident. Tiny, on the other hand, remained on the gallery and was made a hero. Being that Bolo had terrorized the place for so long, and Tiny had handled him for everyone (pretty much), he was never locked up for the fight, nor was he given a misbehavior report for it. From that day on, not only did Tiny have Ant's back, but so did Tiny's workout buddies. It was known throughout the jail, if you messed with Ant, you would catch a proper beatdown. Ant smiled as he replayed the antics in his mind. Now at 18, he was a man, heading to the men's jail. He didn't know why he was being moved so quickly. There were 22-year-olds still being held at the adolescent facility. Whatever the case was, he wasn't one of the ones staying. He didn't know what was in store for him at the next spot, but he prayed he would be as fortunate.

****

Ant walked into the visiting room, jammed packed with inmates and their loved ones. He stopped and tried to catch a glimpse of his visitors. Way off in the back, Ant saw Harold & Denise waving, trying desperately to get his attention. Ant smiled and waved, then proceeded to maneuver the tables to the one Harold & Denise were at. As Ant made his way through the masses, he silently thanked God for the faithfulness and dedication of the Green's. True to their word, they had been with him every step of the way. Now, whatever these two said, Ant never questioned or doubted them.

Just a few steps from the table, they rose to greet Ant. When he finally made it to the table, hugs & kisses were plentiful. After the greetings, all three sat down around the table. "You look good Ant baby. You're growing into a fine black man. If I were a little younger, I might have chosen you over old Harold here." Denise teased both Ant and Harold. Harold looked at Denise with a "yeah, whatever" type of grin on his face. Ant on the other hand, who has always been uncomfortable with his looks, shifted in his seat wishing Denise would leave that subject alone. "Man, you are looking good. You've put on some weight since we've seen you last; you've been working out?" Harold questioned, realizing for the first time that Ant was no longer a child, but a man. Harold looked at Ant with intensity, praying and hoping that all that he had been forced to go through would not plague him the rest of his life. If anyone needed some peace and happiness, it was certainly Ant.

"I try to get some push-ups in every day. They have weights outside, but I only go out when I need to use the phone. I'm not tryna get big no way." And stated, trying to sound at ease talking about his physique. Ant knew for some time now that his looks were both a curse and a gift. "So, what's the deal with this place? You like it better here or the other facility you just left?" Harold inquired, praying that Ant would survive this maximum-security prison.

"If I could go back to the other facility, I'd be out of here now."

"What's the problem here? No one is bothering you, are they?" Denise asked, now serious and willing to walk through the facility and go toe to toe with anyone causing Ant drama. "No, no, it's nothing like that. This place is just different. Plus, I don't know anybody here."

"Ant, this is an adult prison. Men doing hard time. So of course it's gonna be different from where you came from. Also, give it some time. You'll meet some decent folks. Everyone in these places aren't bad" Harold informed Ant. "That's right, just look at you. You aren't bad" commented Denise, bringing a smile to Ant's face.

"What you do is, stay focused on the fact that you're not going to be in this place forever. Then begin to contemplate what you want to do with the rest of your life once you're out." Every time Harold spoke with Ant, he tried to give him positive things to dwell on. He prayed that through his words, the boy would gain a steadfast hope. "Plus, we want you to come live with us in Houston. Our home is your home." Denise stated sincerely as she patted Ant's hand, which was resting on top of the table.

"Well look, we don't have much time left. We have a long drive back to the airport, and there's only one going to Houston tonight." Harold hated leaving Ant; this was the hardest part of visiting, but there was no way around it.

"We left you some food and a few items we thought you could use. You could tell us from time to time what you need; we're in this together, alright honey?" Denise said in a loving, motherly way, that always seemed to touch Ant's heart and replace something that was missing… Sylvia.

"Thank you both. I really do appreciate it. Ant replied, barely able to look them in the eyes, in fear that he would burst into tears. "We know you do. Now we're gonna get out of here. Give us a call tomorrow night, the kids want to talk with you."

"And let us know if there's anything we forgot to bring and we'll send it to you." Denise added.

"Thanks for coming, and yes I will call sometime tomorrow evening." All three stood up and began hugging, first Denise, then Harold. Before Harold removed his arms from around Ant, he said quietly into Ant's ear "give this place a chance to work for you. You did it in the other places, so there is no reason you can't do it here, got it?" Ant shook his head in agreement and said "I got it." Finally, the embrace was broken and Ant proceeded to retrace his steps, the way he had come in. Harold and Denise stood there with their arms around one another, each silently praying for the boy.

"He seems to be holding it together. Quit worrying, he's tough; he'll survive" Denise encouraged her husband, knowing what was troubling him, even before he verbally expressing it. "Yeah, I guess you're right. I'll be glad when he's out though." Harold and Denise gathered their things and headed for the exit. Harold turned once again to the direction Ant had headed, and very quietly asked God to keep and protect Ant.

Chapter 19

"I'll kill you, you punk bitch."

"I got your bitch swinging along wit every female in your family!"

Ant stood listening to the two dudes arguing in the middle of the yard, while waiting his turn to use the phone. He had promised Harold and Denise he would call tonight, and that was the only reason he was in the yard. Ant was the next one up to grab the next available phone. He was inwardly praying that one became available before these two bozos started fighting. Ant had no idea why these two dudes were out here making a scene for the 900 men that were in the yard. One thing was for certain. Both men were furious, and they were just seconds away from going AWOL.

Ant turned his attention away from the verbal feud and thought about asking Harold and Denise for money to purchase a TV. They sent him some things he needed and made sure he had a few dollars in his account to purchase things at the commissary. But a TV, being that they were available and permitted in this facility; that would be nice. Then he thought better of it. Harold and Denise have done way too much as it is, and he needed the little money he saved for when he gets out. He could live without a TV. Plus it might distract him from reading. All of a sudden Ant heard someone yelling like they were in a great deal of pain. Ant turned to where the two dudes had been arguing. The shorter of the two had the dude he was arguing with on the floor, and was stabbing him repeatedly with what looked to be an ice pick. The dude lying on the floor had blood pouring from multiple holes in his face and neck.

A gun shot rang forth. Everyone stopped what they were doing and hit the floor face down. Even those dudes talking on the phone dropped the receivers and went down like lightening. Ant was probably the last one down, but once everyone else hit the deck, he wasted no time. A crew of officers and nurses ran into the yard. The dude with the ice pick was quickly handcuffed and dragged away. The nurses placed the other guy on a stretcher and rushed him in.

No sooner than they had entered the building with the stretcher, an announcement was made on the sound system, "Take it in. Yard are closed." Everyone pushed themselves off the floor and headed towards the building. As Ant made his way toward the building, he wondered if that man would make it as he thought about all the blood. Ant decided right then and there, he was going to stay to himself. He was determined to stay in his cell as much as possible, and work at being invisible. As he entered the building, his mind was bombarded with what he had just witnessed. He realized that the Green family wouldn't be receiving his expected call tonight. Another reality him like a ton of bricks; as long as he was in this situation, there were no certainties… and with that, Ant made his way back to his cell.

****

I've been in the same cell since I arrived here, and this is the only job I've had in this spot." Ant stated, after having completed telling Preme his life story, all the way up to the point where they met.

"Man, in some ways I envy you and in some ways I don't." Preme stated, while scratching his head, still somewhat amazed at all Ant had endured and come through.

"What do you mean?" Ant questioned, totally ignorant to what Preme was expressing.

"What I mean is that I don't envy any of the hell you went through, not one bit. What I do envy is the fact that you went through it like a trooper. Most people would be totally fucked up mentally, but you came out still positive and an all-around better person. I'll tell you one thing, you're better than me." Ant dissected the words Preme was saying and knew there were some hidden hurts there. Ant was determined to get to those hidden things. He couldn't explain why he had to, but something was telling him those things Preme had hidden were extremely deep.

"I'm not a better man than you" Ant retorted, "Placed in the same situation, you would've survived just like I did. Plus, don't get it twisted, you know, from what all I've shared, I've had some major issues, and still do."

"Naw, I know me. And I know for a fact that I couldn't have handled all that like you did, nor would I have come out of the situation being a good individual, such as yourself.

"I still say you would've done the same. People are always quick to say what they could have or wouldn't have done, when in all actuality they never have or never will experience certain situations." Ant had no idea as to why he was pushing Preme in this type of dialogue. Ant didn't get the notion that Preme was abused, but there was something there. That's the only way Ant could describe it, and Ant didn't think his notion was wrong.

"Ant, until a person tells you their experience, you can't assume anything. You're smart, but you ain't that damn smart. And I'm telling you, I know I wouldn't have handled the situation the way you did." Preme finally finished barking, took a deep breath, put his head down and rubbed his hands over his still tightly braided hair. Ant was shocked and stunned at Preme's reply. He began to really question himself… was it really smart to push him, because there was no telling how Preme would react or respond. Ant thought of the old saying one of the elder women of the church would say "In for a penny, in for a pound."

"Who was it?" Ant questioned. Just mere moments ago, Ant didn't believe that Preme was abused, but now it didn't seem too far-fetched. Knowing his question would catch him off guard, Ant hoped it would thrust him into a confession.

"Who was what" Preme asked in response to Ant's question, with a look of bewilderment on his face.

"Who was it that violated you?"

"Violated me? What the fuck are you talking about?"

"Who was it that abused you? Was it a relative?" Ant asked, but was totally prepared for the response he received.

"I thought you were smart" Preme began saying through clenched teeth, "but you're a sick mofo."

"What the hell are you talking about?" Ant interrupted, only to be silenced by Preme.

"You think everyone has been through the very same thing you have, don't you?" Preme was furious and even though his voice was low, Ant could tell it was being done through great effort. "Just like you think every male that befriends you, wants to sex you. You thought that about me remember?"

"Preme look…"

"No, you look. I told you before that you need to stop being so damn closed minded; you limit not only your thinking that way, but your possibilities as well." Preme wasn't even sure if he was making sense, but Ant had pissed him off to degrees unknown, and he had to vent. Otherwise, he was gonna go postal. "Furthermore" Preme continued, "like I stated earlier, I'm not you. I was never violated, as you put it. The first time a wacko pervert would have come to me, rest assure ,I would have bodied that ass. See I believe that God helps those who help themselves."

"So, you're saying that because I didn't kill the bastard, or try to kill him, that God refused to help me?" Now it was Ant's turn to get peeved.

"I'm not speaking for you Ant, I'm speaking for me. So if it don't apply, let it fly."

"That's what you say now, but you didn't say God helps you. You said those, meaning the rest of us humans."

"Well, let me rephrase that for your sensitive ass, no pun intended. God will help me because I help myself. Better?" Preme responded sarcastically.

"You know Preme, you can be a real asshole at times." Ant stated with disgust shown on his face and heard in his voice.

"It takes one to know one, never 68 and owe one." Rapped Preme, realizing that he hadn't listened to his Lil' Kim "Hardcore" cassette in a minute, and made a mental note to thump that asap. Ant realized right then and there that Preme was just trying to get under his skin; he wasn't upset anymore, but rather just trying to repay him for what he had done to him a moment ago. Ant decided he wasn't falling for it.

"You know what Preme? It's late and I'm gonna crash. You enjoy the rest of your night." Ant got up from his spot at the gate and fell back on his bed.

"Yeah, you have a good night too. With your sensitive ass."

"Whatever." Ant replied as he laid there staring at the ceiling. As Ant laid there, he heard Preme moving around in his cell, more than likely getting ready for bed. Ant began to rehash the conversation with Preme and his reaction to his question about him being abused. For the life of him, Ant couldn't grasp what was going on with Preme. Still racking his brain, ain't finally dozed off, while Preme was in bed, headphones on, blasting Lil' Kim.

****

Saturday morning, after feeding the keep-locks and removing their trays and garbage, Ant told CO Simmons that he was going back to bed until lunch. Once Ant was in his cell, the gate closed and Ant fell back on the bed, and was asleep in minutes. An hour later Ant abruptly awoke from his sleep when his cell opened. Ant looked at his watch, knowing it couldn't possibly be lunch time that quickly. Sure enough, it was only 8:05 am. Ant got out of bed and stepped out the cell, looking to the front of the gallery for CO Simmons. When Simmons saw Ant step out of the cell, he yelled down the gallery to him; "Morgan, visit."

Ant stood there rubbing his eyes, unbelieving what he had just heard. No one came to visit him other than Harold and Denise, and they always informed him as to when they were coming. Everyone else he knew wrote letters. Ant had met quite a few people through the various ministries that came in for service. Some he knew from when he was home, who wrote and some he even called from time to time. He couldn't think of anyone who would just decide to pay him a visit. Ant went in his cell, gathered the things he needed for his shower. With that done, he stepped out of his cell and thought of Preme. Preme was always pulling off surprises and this could very well be the doing of him. Ant went next door to Preme's cell, and found him laid on his back, mouth open and snoring softly.

Preme, get up." Ant demanded, however, Preme just grunted and turned on his side still asleep. Ant put his hand through the bars and hit the bed lightly a few times. Preme sat straight up, just as Ant did when his cell opened up while he was sleeping.

"Yo, what time is it?"

"It's 9:00 am."

"Man, I'm going back to sleep" stated Preme, who laid back down, this time taking his pillow and placing it over his face.

"They just called me for a visit." Preme removed the pillow from his face and asked "well what the hell are you doing standing here? Go see your peoples."

"That's the thing, I don't know who it is. You didn't send anyone up here to see me, did you?" Ant asked.

"Why the hell would I do that? I ain't trying to embarrass myself," Preme joked.

"You woke up with jokes this morning I see, but is it possible that you can be serious for about 60 seconds?"

"Look Ant, I haven't the faintest idea as to who came to see you. My guess is that Harold and Denise wanted to surprise you." Ant thought about what Preme had just stated, and realized that it was the most logical explanation.

"You know, you're probably right. Let me go get ready." Ant said as he took off to the front of the gallery where the showers are located. Twenty-Five minutes later, Ant checked himself out in the mirror. With a beige Eddie Bauer, long sleeved button down, Timbs to match and a plain pair of Chanel frames on (all compliments of Preme), he was pleased with what he saw. Ant put down the mirror and headed out the cell.

"Let me see what you're sporting" Preme said, who was waiting on the gate for Ant to come out. Ant stepped over in front of Preme's cell, still adjusting his belt and pants. "Not bad son, not bad. But you're missing two things." Preme left the gate for a moment and returned with a small plastic bottle in his hands, which Ant knew held scented Muslim oil. "This is not what you think, this is the real thing." Ant took the cap off and New West filled his nostrils. Ant placed some on his hand and rubbed it over his shirt. He knew better than to ask where he had gotten the cologne from.

"What's the other thing that I'm missing?" Ant asked, after giving the bottle back.

"This." Preme said as he produced a platinum 18" chain, with a matching cross. Ant was in complete awe of the jewelry. Not only was it beautiful, but he could just imagine what it cost.

"Yo, I can't wear that. That's…" Ant paused, unable to find the words, but he found one "Yours", unable to come up with anything better.

"No, it's not mine anymore. It's yours." Preme said as Ant took the chain and cross in his hands, still not believing it was there. I've never even worn this piece. I got more stuff than I could possibly ever use. Now put it on and get out of here. Someone's downstairs waiting on you." Ant looked up from being held captive from the shine. His eyes were glossy, showing signs of eruption. Thank you, just didn't seem adequate. Preme was searching for the words to express his gratitude. "I know you're grateful and the whole nine. Now put the thing on and go. You's a hard-headed lil' bastard!" Preme joked, which brought a smile to Ant's face. Ant slid the chain around his neck and sped off to the front of the gallery. Ant thought of a lone song they used to sing in church. It simply said "you're latter will be greater than your past." And Ant had a feeling that everything was going to be alright.

Chapter 20

Twenty minutes later, after being patted down, frisked and processed, Ant stood at the entrance of the already crowded visiting room looking for Harold and Denise. Ant looked throughout the entire room and saw no signs of either of them. There were only two tables that didn't have a prisoner at them; one was a very obese white woman with her three black children, who seemed to be arguing over the food items that were laid out on the table. Ant knew she couldn't possibly be here to see him. The other was a Hispanic male, sporting a tight Dolce & Gabbana zippered sweater that Ant recognized from a recent GW magazine. Ant was certain the dude wasn't here to see him. Just as Ant was about to turn and walk back to where he was processed, the man stood up and began waving. Ant pointed to himself and looked around the at the same time, but clearly asking the man "Who me?" The guy shook his head and waved Ant to come over.

Ant scratched his head and began walking over to where the brother was standing next to the table. As Ant got closer, he realized that there was something very familiar about the brother. With about twelve feet left to reach the table, the brother began to smile, and that's when it hit Ant. Ant picked up his pace, and when he got to the table, he stopped and looked closely at the guy who just stood there smiling. Obviously enjoying and savoring Ant's bewilderment. Finally, Ant spoke: "This can't be Culo?"

"Well, that's what I used to go by 10 years ago, now it's just Manny. Ant still in shock, remembered that Culo had written his name in the back of his Bible "Manuel Reyes".

But this couldn't be the same kid that sucked dick day in and day out back in Mod 6. Ant rushed forward and embraced Culo... rather Manny. When the embrace had ended, it was Ant who spoke.

"What the hell are you doing here?"

"Duh, I'm here to see you, you big dummy." Manny responded to Ant, stealing that old line from Sanford & Son. "Let's sit down, and I'll tell you everything."

"Man, you are looking good Ant. You done put on some weight and all that. I'm really glad you survived this madness."

"Yeah, it's finally just about over. But you got it going on with the gear, and I see that bling on your arm." Ant said pointing to the diamond and platinum bracelet that hung on Manny's arm.

"Yeah, God has been good to me, in spite of me... but we'll get to that later. So, how are you?" Manny asked, dropping the smile.

"I'm doing good, and like you said, God is good. How did you find me?"

"The almighty power of the internet. I told you I would track you down if I didn't hear from you. And so, here I am." Manny responded with a huge grin on his face.

"Forgive me for not writing, but I was just working so hard to survive this place. If I wrote 10 letters these past ten years, then I wrote a lot" Ant stated, hoping Manny would not hold it against him.

"Don't worry about it man, I understand. Plus, when I first went home, I was out of control" Manny confessed.

"Man, what happened? This ain't the same individual that was with me in Mod 6, the one who saved my life" said Ant, remembering the night he tried to end it all.

"Man, so much has happened, I don't even know where to begin."

"How did you get here?" Ant asked.

"I took the bus, so I need to be outside at 2:45." Manny answered. "That gives us just over 4 hrs., so go for it." Ant took one of the sodas that was on the table, popped the top, took a swallow and sat back in the chair.

"A few days after you left, I found out that I had passed the GED exam, and I received my diploma. I told myself that I was gonna go out there, get a job and enroll in a trade school. Maybe learn how to do hair. I was already an expert at head, so I figured doing hair would be a breeze." Manny said, cracking a smile, but that lasted for only a second. Manny turned serious, took one of the sodas, opened it and took a long swallow. Ant decided to let Manny go at his own pace, with limited interruptions from him. Manny placed the soda back on the table and proceeded on with his story.

"The day I was released, I took the bus to Port Authority. By the end of the ride, I had my plan laid out." Manny paused and Ant could tell the memories and the things he was about to share was going to be extremely painful. "I got off the bus and was strutting through Port Authority when this blue-black dude, with a body like Arnold and a face like Denzel, pressed me. He was flirting, and you know my hot, young ass was too." For a second, Ant saw a glimpse of Culo, but he sat quietly taking in all that Manny was saying. "He told me his name was Horse, and I told him my handle. He started smiling, looking me up and down." Manny paused for a second, took a deep breath and then pressed on.

"Horse told me that he had a room around the corner and some good weed… I was more than welcome to join him. Horse took my bag, and we walked around the corner to his room. His room was very neat and clean, which was surprising compared to how the outside of the building looked. He had a bed, no chairs, a small color TV, hot plate and mad clothes." Manny stopped and got up out of his seat.

"Where the hell are you going?" Ant asked, thinking Manny had lost his mind.

"I'm going to run over to the vending machine and get some of those hot wings, before that big heifer over there with the torpedo tits buys all of them. What do you want?" Manny asked, already pulling money from his pockets.

"Wings are good. And get some fries too."

"Gotcha" Manny said, and took off towards the vending machines. While Manny was gone, Ant wondered what he was in store for when he heard the rest of Manny's story. Did any of it have to do with him? Or was this Manny's way of purging himself. Before Ant could contemplate any longer, Manny was back with an armful of food. "I got a little of everything, cause Roseanne Barr over there is buying everything. I think she's gonna smuggle some of that food out in her torpedo tits." Manny sat down and Ant could tell he was ready to pick up where he left off.

"Feel free to eat whenever you're ready. Now, where was I?"

"You had just gotten to Horse's room."

"Yeah, okay. We sat down on the bed. He had some music playing, produced a forty and we began to sip. While we were sitting and sipping, he pulled some weed from under the mattress. Before he rolled the weed in the blunt, from out of nowhere he pulled a small bag of coke and began lacing the weed with it. Are you still with me?" Manny asked Ant.

"Of course I am. You have my undivided attention. Continue." Ant responded.

"Alright, we began smoking, mind you. I had never smoked weed and coke, but I was feeling what it did to me. The next thing I knew, Horse had his cock in his hand stroking it. I knew right then and there why they called him Horse." Manny put his hand on his heart and shook his head as he remembered the event. Manny's theatrics brought a smile to his face... within seconds, Manny had gone back to Culo, and back to Manny again. "Well, you know how hot my ass was back then. I looked at Horse and said, "Why jerk it and waste it, when I can suck it and taste it." From there, it was on. I won't bore you with all those details." Manny stated, knowing good and well those details weren't boring, but Ant didn't want to hear all that.

"I never made it home that day. I did make it the next day, but I was already addicted to drugs again, as well as Horse. I didn't pursue none of the positive things I had planned to do. I ended up getting kicked out of my house, and ended up staying with Horse." Manny paused, removed a chicken wing from the tray in front of him and began to nibble on it with a faraway look on his face. When he had finished the wing, he placed the bones on a napkin, wiped his mouth and continued talking. "Like they always say, there's a price for everything. Horse had no other job than being a professional hustler. He would rob, steal, beg and even sell his ass to whomever would pay. And there were many who paid for that body; I know, because I watched him handle tricks many days. Horse then told me that I had to earn my stay, so he put me to work. I would seduce drug dealers and then take their drugs. Get old white men in the bed, wear them out and run off with their money. I did it all. At least twice a week, I was the featured guest for a group of two, three, four, and one time five men. I was sinking rapidly."

Manny took a napkin from the table and dried his tear stained cheeks. Ant could feel Manny's pain. He wanted Manny to know that it wasn't important to him that he finish the story. "Manny, you don't have to finish this. If it's causing you too much pain, we can talk about something else."

Manny began shaking his head no, "No, I need to tell it; it's a part of the healing process, so let me get it out." Manny sternly said.

"Okay, I got it. Go forth."

More controlled now, Manny proceeded, "One morning, after a long night of hoeing, I came home to find the room empty. Everything was gone, with the exception of the bed. All his clothes, my clothes and my money were gone. I didn't cry or anything at first; I laid down on the bed, thinking this was some kind of sick joke. I must've dosed off, because the next I knew, I was being awakened by the manager. He told me that I had to leave immediately, because they needed to clean the place before the new tenants got there... and they were due in thirty minutes." Ant knew that was the point in which Manny had hit rock bottom.

"I had nowhere to go, no contacts, and about $220.00 in my pocket. I went to the nearest crack dealer, copped and got high. I repeated the same process until the money was gone. I lived on the streets for days with no food, no shower, nothing. At first, I was still able to turn a trick or two. But I had gotten so scary looking and smelly that I couldn't pay anyone to be with me." Manny took a long swallow from the soda can that sat on the table in front of him. After downing the contents, he looked at each can as if to say "damn, I wish this was something else much, much stronger." "I'm not boring you, am I?" Manny asked, knowing he needed to bring the story in before Ant gets up and leaves him sitting there in the visiting room alone.

"No Manny. I want to hear this, just as much as you need to tell it" responded Ant, hoping that he had reassured Manny that he was really concerned and not just nosey.

"About two weeks after I had been out on the street, I propositioned this old white man. I told him he could be with me for the night, if he had the money. Mind you, now I'm smelling like a sewer, breath kicking and all. He asks me how much, and I told him $100. I knew I was pushing it, because I was tore up from the floor up! But he said okay, gave me $50 up front, and told me he'd give me another $50 at his house." This time, Ant had to interrupt.

"Manny, don't tell me you went home with this dude?"

"Ant, that's what whores do. And that's what I was doing. In my mind, I was saying, I'll go to his house, rob his ass for everything he's got."

"Weren't you fearful for your life?" Ant asked.

"Man, that wasn't living. I was a dead man walking… so no, I wasn't fearful. Now, let me finish up. I'm almost there." By Manny's tone and eagerness to finish the story, plus the fact that he was sitting here looking like a million bucks, let Anthony know that the worst of Manny's story was over. "We got in his car, which was a banging Audi. It seems to be the typical car for the rich but modest white folks." Manny stated with humor, which caused him and Ant to chuckle and nod in agreement. "We were in the car, and I was trying to fondle him and the whole nine, but he kept telling me to wait until we got home. Cool, I sat back and took my tired ass to sleep. When I woke up, we were in front of a brownstone; I later found out I was in Brooklyn. Now, check this. We go inside, and I flop on the nearest chair which was in the living room. He tells me he'll be right back. I don't know how long he was gone, but when he came back, someone was with him; a woman." Ant didn't expect that, and simply got tired of trying to piece the story together before he heard it.

"It was his wife. They both looked to be in their 60's. When she came in the room carrying a tray, I went off. I started yelling 'I don't do no freak shows with women', I was completely going off. She sat the tray down on the table, and low and behold, it was food. They must have seen my longing, because they both said in unison "eat" … and I ate like there was no damn tomorrow. Manny stopped and looked at his watch, seeing how much time was left before the visit would end. Seeing that they had about 90 minutes left, Manny left the backroads and got on the expressway. "To make a long story short, they didn't want any sexual favors; they wanted someone they could care for. They had been married going on 45 years, and were never able to have kids of their own. They are good law abiding, church going Baptists, that really lived what they preach." Manny started getting really choked up, talking about this couple. Ant silently thanked God for sending someone Manny's way to rescue him.

"Their names are Stan and Janice Mitchell. Stan started a cleaning service right before he married Janice; and it became a multi-million-dollar business. After I was clean, Stan showed me the ropes. And three years ago, I took over. Five months later, Stan passed away. And thirteen months after that, Janice passed. They left me everything." Ant couldn't believe his ears, and couldn't keep silent.

"Manny! Only God could turn all of what you've been through around like that! Nobody but Jesus!"

"I know that's right! I went to church faithfully with Stan and Janice, and during a revival one night, I gave my life to the Lord. This had to be no more than six or seven months from the time they took me in. I don't claim to be the best saint, but I'm sure not what I used to be."

"None of us are, and if you find anyone who says they are, they ain't nothing but a lying wonder." Ant said sternly.

"Boy, you better preach! You getting ready to make me jump up and do the Holy cabbage patch in here!" Declared Manny, who even though he sounded like he was playing; was dead ass serious.

"No, I ain't preaching. I'm just speaking the truth."

"That you are my brother. That you are. There is one more thing I have to tell you, but you might want to hold on to your seat for this one." Ant couldn't think of anything else this guy could say to shock him; he was convinced that he had heard it all.

"Alright, let me have it."

"Since that night that I gave my life to the Lord…" Manny paused, stretching Ant's curiosity to the limit. However, Ant didn't say a word… he was anxiously awaiting the rest of the story. "Since that night, I haven't been with another man sexually." Ant was about to fall out of his chair in shock. Knowing how Manny used to be, only God could deliver and keep him. "And I'm engaged to be married to a wonderful and supportive woman named Susan. Yes, with a name like Susan, you know she's white. She works at my company, knows all about my past, and still wants to marry me… go figure." Manny stated playfully.

Ant was sincerely overjoyed for Manny, and couldn't help but give God the praise for what he had done in his friend's life. "I'm not gonna sit here and lie. I struggle at times with the old me, but God's word tells me that I am more than a conqueror. And I stand on that. This new life that he has given me, I refuse to mess it up." By this time, Manny and Ant were both in tears, and they didn't care who saw them either.

"Man, I don't know what to say, other than; look what the Lord has done. To him be all the glory!"

"Amen my brother. Amen."

"Why did you decide to come see me now?" Ant asked, knowing they didn't have much more time left before the visit had to end.

"Two reasons: First, I know you're coming home soon. So I wanted to let you know that whatever you need, Susan and I are here for you all the way. You need a home, a job, money, whatever, we got you. You don't have to make any decisions now, just think about it and let me know."

"And the second reason?" A curious Ant was anxious to know.

"The second reason is I was given a message to relay to you."

"A message from who?" Ant was really curious now.

"From the Lord. He told me to tell you that your latter will be greater than your past." Immediately, Ant felt the presence of the Lord just fill him and he began to tremble in his presence. "He said to tell you, just as He did for me, He will surely do for you, for He is no respecter of persons." Tears unashamedly ran down Ant's face, at hearing the message from the Lord. Ant had tried not to worry about his return to society, but deep down, he was frightened. It had been a long ten years of incarceration, and now he was finally going to be released. He was 15-years-old when he was arrested, and now he was 25. So very much had changed. But most of all, Ant had changed.

"I hope those are tears of joy, for this is the day that the Lord has made. You need to rejoice and be glad." Manny declared, voice raising a little and even clapping his hands at the end of the sentence to emphasize his point. "Man, I gotta calm down before I lose my cool, up in here, up in here!" Manny stated, fanning himself, trying to calm the fire within. Ant hadn't uttered a word since Manny told him what thus sayeth the Lord. It was extremely hard for Ant to get himself together. It had been such a long time since God had spoken to him like that.

"Manny, you don't know what it means to me to hear God speak, especially through you. I always knew God had a purpose for you" Ant finally stated, once he had found his voice again.

"I know. Who would've thought right?"

"Ten minutes left on all visits." Declared a voice over the sound system. "Look Ant, we only have ten minutes, so listen up. I brought you some food, and I'll send more next month. Enough to last you until your release. Send me your sizes and I'll send you some decent gear to walk out in. And think about my offer too. We have plenty of room at the house for you, as well as the office."

"Manny, I don't know what to say; you are God sent, and I thank you. I will write you and let you know what the deal is."

"Alright, let me get a head start out of here before the rush begins. Ant, my numbers and address are in the package. I'll be looking to hear from you in the upcoming weeks. Let's have a quick word of prayer." The two joined hands and bowed their heads. It was Manny who prayed. *"Lord, we thank you for bringing us together once again. Please continue to keep Ant and order his steps when he is released. We thank you, and we give you glory, in Jesus' name, Amen."* With that, they both stood and embraced.

"God bless you man" Ant said as they were in the embrace.

"Like wise my brother, like wise." They broke from the embrace and Manny grabbed his belongings from the table. Heading for the exit he turned around one more time to wave at Ant, who waved back. Ant turned and made his way over to the room where all the inmates had to be stripped searched at the completion of each visit. While in route back to his cell, Ant was blown away by this entire visit with Manny. It amazed him how God always supplied what he needed when he needed it. Who wouldn't serve a God like that?!

<u>Chapter 21</u>

After being searched and picking up the package that Manny had left, Ant slowly made his way back to the gallery struggling to balance the four bags of food. As he made his way back, he began to think on all the times he had doubted and questioned God. Every single time he had doubt, God always did the miraculous and it always shut Ant up. After a 15-minute walk, that would normally take three minutes, Ant had made it back to the gallery. "You sure got a lot of stuff there. The man upstairs must be really feeling you these days." Officer Simmons said as he opened the gate leading to the gallery. Ant chuckled at Simmons' use of the word "feeling". It bugged Ant out how white folks were always jackin' our slang.

"So, who was it that came to see you and bless you with all that food?" Simmons asked.

"An old friend I haven't seen or heard from in ten years; we had a really good visit."

"That's good, I'm happy for you. Lock in for now. The next shift will be here in a few. I'll tell them to lock you out immediately." With that, Ant made his way down to his already opened cell. The gallery was extremely quiet and Ant could hear Preme softly snoring. Ant placed his bags on the floor and laid back on his bed. He was way too wired to take a nap… plus, it didn't make sense because his cell would be opening any moment. So, he just laid there and thought about the day's events.

Getting up from the bed, Ant searched for his mirror. When he located it, he sat back down on the bed. He took the mirror, looked into it, and immediately the platinum cross and chain reflected brightly. Ant had worn the chain inside his shirt during the visit because he didn't want to draw any attention to himself. His free hand went to the cross and began caressing the precious metal. The design of both pieces was a style he had never seen before, and there was no doubt in his mind that they were both one of a kind. They were probably created by Harry Winston or Jacob the Jeweler, knowing how deep Preme's pockets are. Ant placed the mirror on top of his TV and began thinking about Manny. He thought back to when he had first met him in Mod 6 as Culo, and how he was an out of control teen trying to swallow everything he could. Now, ten years later, he's been transformed, delivered and redeemed.

Just then Ant's cell opened. He got up still dressed in his visit gear, stepped onto the gallery and made his way to the front. There was some garbage that had not been disposed of, due to the fact that he was on a visit. Once he had taken care of the garbage, he made his way back down the gallery. It was still too early for the evening meal, so he passed his cell and stopped in front of Preme's who was still knocked out on his back… snoring. Ant had never been one to wake someone when they're sleeping, however… he had done so this morning and he could no longer hold in what happened today. He had to share it. Ant kicked the bottom of the cell gate with his boot. "Rise and shine." Ant yelled, as Preme jumped and sat straight up in his bed.

"You just now getting back?" Preme asked, as he rubbed his eyes with one hand and looked at his watch on the other.

"I've been back about a half-hour, but you were still over here snoring.

"I don't snore" Preme declared, rising from the bed. Then he grabbed his toothbrush and began brushing his teeth in the small sink.

"Whatever" Ant responded.

"Who came to see you?" Preme asked, once he completed his brushing. He sat back down on his bed, still not looking full awake.

"Take a wild guess."

"Harold and Denise?"

"I said a wild guess; come on… think wild!"

"Shadrack?"

The smile that was on Ant's face faded quickly upon hearing Preme's guess. "That's not even funny. I said think wild, not stupid! And before you have another brainstorm, no it wasn't Sylvia either!"

"Well, I don't know. Why don't you just go ahead and tell me; I was never one for games." Ant believed full and well that Preme knew that if Shadrack had indeed showed up, he would not be standing there right now. Upon first sight, Ant would've opened a case of whoop ass on that mofo. Yeah, Ant knew that because he's saved he's supposed to forgive others… even Shadrack. However, he wasn't that saved, not yet anyway.

"It was Culo!" Ant said with a huge smile plastered on his face.

"Correct me if I'm wrong but, isn't Culo the one that was on the Rock cleaning everyone's pipes? Isn't he the one that found you when you slit your wrists?" Preme asked, scratching his head, looking bewildered.

"That's the one. But he no longer goes by the name Culo... his name is Manny.

"So, he's no longer ass huh? Go figure. I say once ass, always ass." Preme stated, then began to laugh at his own antics. Ant let the last comment slide, and took the next 25 minutes telling Preme all about the visit. "Damn, that's deep! He's straight now, and engaged to be married to a real broad and has crazy bank huh?" Preme asked, sincerely surprised and happy; because Ant was.

"Yeah, it seems that way." Just then, the keep-locks dinner arrived and Ant needed to hand them out. "The feeds are up here. I'll be back once I hand them all out. I already know you don't want your tray."

"Well check it. I'm going back to bed. Holla at me later on."

"Alright. That will give me some time to put the food away that Manny brought me."

"Yeah well, make sure you leave some of it on the gate for me when I wake up; leave my cut... ya heard."

"Whatever" Ant replied, and then took off down the gallery, feeling as light as a feather.

****

Later that night, about 2 am, the gallery was quiet with the exception of various tones of snoring. Ant laid on the bed with his eyes closed still full from the meal he and Preme had eaten four hours ago, and thinking about his visit with Manny. The midnight CO was quietly making his round, looking in every cell. Everyone on the gallery was sleep thought the CO, except for Preme, who had been waiting for the CO to make his round. The CO got in front of Preme's cell and began looking around as if something had changed in the last thirty seconds. Ant laid as still as he possibly could with his eyes slightly cracked, taking in the happenings. The CO went into his pants pocket, removed his cell phone and handed it between the bars to Preme.

"Do not answer, should the other line ring; just ignore it. Handle your business and I'll be back for it in twenty-minutes" the CO stated, and was about to walk away when Preme responded.

"Make it thirty"

"I said twenty"

Preme grabbed the CO's shirt through the bars, and with clenched teeth he spoke trying hard to control his anger. "You'll get this phone back when I'm finished with it. If it wasn't for me, you'd still be on the street smoking rock. Now you wanna front on me you bitch ass, trick ass punk? Get out of my face." Preme said as he shoved the CO, who then took off down the gallery. Preme sat down on the bed and dialed a number that began with a 718-area code… Brooklyn.

****

While Ant was laying on his bed reminiscing about his surprise visit with Manny, Peaches was in the kitchen of his Clinton Hills apartment fixing a tray of wine and cheese. Clad with a fresh perm, wearing a red silk robe with a see-through cherry red thong on, Peaches hoped the wine and cheese would serve as an aphrodisiac for the second round in the sack. As Peaches sliced the cheese, he hummed the chorus of an old SWV song "Downtown". While humming, he thought about how good his life was going. He had a fab apartment, clothes, jewelry galore and a flashy, yet outdated ride. If he could just come up with some "loose change", he could cop that new Range Rover he had seen advertised; he'd really be the Queen Bitch then.

At that precise moment, Peaches heard his cell phone ring somewhere in the distance. Peaches rushed out of the kitchen into the living room where the phone was resting on his onyx & ivory glassed topped coffee table. Peaches was running so fast that he ran smack dab into the leg of the table with his toes, causing him to cry out in anguish. "You alright babe?" The Ja Rule look alike yelled out from the bedroom. Peaches flopped down on the sofa not knowing what to grab; the still ringing phone or his bruised toe. "Yea, I'm alright. Just lay back and get some rest. I'll be back in there in just a few seconds" Peaches said as he grabbed the phone. Whoever this is on the phone was about to get the business from Peaches. There was just no damn excuse for anyone to be calling him at 2 am. Even if someone had died, there was nothing he could do about it in the middle of the night. Might as well wait until the morning.

"This better be good" Peaches said into the phone, upon answering it.

"I have a job for you Peaches. A well-paying job." It had been some time since Peaches heard the voice on the line, but it was one that he could never forget. The voice represented both money and power. Peaches quickly lost the attitude.

"The last time we met, you told me you wouldn't be needing my services again."

"Well, things have changed. Has our friend contacted you since we last spoke?"

"Yes. He contacted me a few months after, when I was still living with my moms" Peaches confessed.

"What did he say?"

"He wanted to know if he could see me and Precious again. He also said that as much as he hated missing me, that he really and truly does."

"And what did you tell him?"

"I cussed his fat ass out, and told him to never call me again. And so far, he hasn't."

"So, you cussed him out huh?" "Like I always do."

"Typical Peaches. I need you to contact him."

"Here we go with this bullshit again. I thought you had everything you needed the last time."

"Look Peaches, I don't have a lot of time. If you're willing to do this, go to my store in Mid-Town and they'll give you all the gear you need for that fat bastard and his wife as bait. Plus, you can pick out some pieces for yourself."

"That's it?" Peaches asked, not believing this was all he was offering.

"If you'd let me finish bitch, you'll see that there's more."

"Okay, I'm listening." Peaches said, totally ignoring being called a bitch. Had it been anyone else, Peaches would have verbally tongue lashed them. But one did not want to tangle with this mofo; he'd run through you like Hurricane George did to the Florida coast.

"Now, there will be $75,000 for you and $25,000 for Precious, if you can get him in on it. So, are you down?

The new Range quickly came to Peaches mind. With $75,000 he could even get it custom painted. What a babe he'd be, pushing that... he'd probably have to push the thugs off they'd be so into him. And into him was a good thing. "Yeah, I'm in. What I gotta do?" Ten minutes later, after all the details had been hashed out, Peaches was ready to get back to his Ja Rule in the bedroom who was probably asleep by now. "Alright, I will get started on this. First thing in the morning and I'll await your call."

"One other thing Peaches. When you get to the shop to pick up the gear, stop by CIA records and see Michael Richards..."

"You just want me to waltz into CIA Records headquarters and request to see the president? They'll throw my faggot ass out on my ears!"

"Bitch! If I'm telling you to do it, just trust me. Tell him I'm sending him a tape and then I'll be sending him someone real soon. Tell him to give him the red-carpet treatment; no bogus deals and promotion... and no bogus producer. Tell him that I'll check him when I can. Got it?"

"Yeah, I got it. You are doing a lot of shot calling from behind bars." Peaches shut up immediately, regretting what he just said.

"Yes I am. I can even get a bitch knocked off if I so choose; would you like to call my bluff?"

"No. I'll call Precious in the morning. Rest assured; . business will be handled."

"I know it will." With that, Preme hung up the phone, and left Peaches listening to the dial tone.

****

ChoirBoy

After a long night of riding the pony, then having to make him breakfast, around 10 am Peaches sent his friend on his way. He pulled out his phone book, grabbed his phone and was ready to work. Peaches dialed the first number on his list for Precious, which was to his New Jersey home. Precious answered on the third ring.

"Precious in the house."

"What's goin' on heifer? You can't call nobody?" Peaches asked

"Peaches?"

"Who else bitch?"

"What's good? I hate to tell you, I only have about ten minutes to talk; I'm on my way to the airport."

"And where are you off to, might I ask?

"Cancun baby! And his name is Malik. You might know him. He's from Brooklyn too." Precious stated, knowing Peaches was going to ask.

"How long will you be gone for?"

"Two weeks. Okay, what's goin' on? I know when you start asking questions, you have something up your sleeve."

"How would you like to make $15,000 in one night?"

"Talk bitch. I'm interested."

"You remember Shadrack?"

"Not the Rev. again?"

"But not only him. He has a preacher friend named Willie Laeitgood."

"You know what? I'm not even gonna ask. Just tell me when and where?"

"I'll set it up for some time when you get back from Cancun. How does that sound?"

"The fifteen is what sounds good. Okay then, I'll holla when I get back."

"Talk to you then." Peaches replied and hung up the phone. Peaches wondered if he should feel bad about cheating Precious out of ten thousand dollars, but he quickly dismissed the thought. "A bitch gotta do, what a bitch gotta do. Now, moving right along" Peaches said to himself. The next matter of business was handled with no problem. Peaches had called the boutique to see what they had waiting so that when he called Shadrack, he could tell him what to expect as far as clothes go.

Peaches decided to call Shadrack to see when he'd be interested in meeting. Peaches found the number and just looked at it for a moment, trying to mentally prepare himself to deal with Shadrack's antics. He also knew Shadrack would certainly be surprised to hear from him, especially since he was probably too drunk to remember giving him the number. Then, there was the fact that Shadrack had called his house after the last episode, and the caller ID brightly displayed Shadrack's number. Picking up the phone, realizing ain't nothin' to it but to do it... Peaches dialed the number.

"Grace and peace be unto. This is the Rev. Shadrack E. Brown, how can I bless you this morning?" Shadrack sang into the phone, after picking it up in the midst of the second ring.

"Yeah, whateva nucca. I got some rare goods for you and the Mrs., are you interested in setting up a meeting?"

Peaches sound off, knowing Shadrack would know something was up if he wasn't his naturally abrupt and foul-mouthed self."

"Brother Maurice, is that…"

"Listen you fat, triflin, having bigger titties than Pamela Anderson Lee, stupid prick. I've told you once and I've told you twice, my name is Peaches, not Maurice. And I certainly ain't your brother, or do you suck your brother's cock too?" Peaches was not pretending to be pissed; he really was. This mofo had a way of bringing out that side of him.

"Well Peaches, you caught me at a good time. The Mrs. is in Toronto on a retreat, and won't be back for a couple of weeks. So, tell me about these rare goods.

Peaches began rattling off all the various items that he had been informed of (when he called the boutique), were awaiting his pick-up. "Mm… I'd say you've been really busy. You've acquired all the things that I've desired. Now, are your prices reasonable?" Shadrack asked, sounding like he was in the pulpit preaching a Sunday morning message."

"Aren't they always?" Peaches asked sarcastically, but pushed on before Shadrack had a chance to respond. "You remember my sister Precious?"

"Of course I do. How could I forget. Will he be joining us for our next meeting?" Shadrack asked, barely able to contain his excitement.

"That could be arranged, but it depends on you."

"How so?"

"Well, I really wanted to make this meeting special, being that it's been so long since we've seen each other. I was thinking, why don't you bring your buddy Willie what's his name?"

"You mean Laeitgood?"

"Yeah, him."

"This is starting to sound like something! However, my dear, if Willie agrees to come, which I'm sure he'd love the idea, he won't be able to come for at least three weeks to a month."

"Well, that's fine because Precious is away for the next two weeks on business. Plus by that time, I'm certain that I'll have some more items that you'll be interested in."

"So, let's set the calendar for four weeks. We'll meet like we always do, on a Friday, and you'll make all the arrangements, right?"

"Yes, as always."

"Alright Peaches. I look forward to seeing you and Precious, as I'm sure Laeitgood will also. I'll call you if there's any changes, which I don't foresee.

"Okay Rev., take care, and see you in four. Don't forget to bring the cash."

"Oh, I won't forget to bring anything. Until then." Shadrack, pressed the disconnect button on his phone, held it for a moment and then released it. Once he had a dial tone, he pressed one button and automatically speed dial did its job. On the fourth ring, there was an answer.

"Praise the Lord! The Rev. Laeitgood here at your service" answered Laeitgood.

ChoirBoy

"Willie, you and I are going to New York!" Willie was all ears.

****

Once the conversation with Shadrack was over, Peaches replaced the phone and went looking for his checkbook, which was on his night stand in the bedroom. "I think I'll take a drive to the Range dealers and maybe, I'll place my order." Peaches said out loud, knowing good and well, he was purchasing his truck today.

****

It was dark when Peaches returned to his apartment. He was laden with bags of lime green clothing to match the lime green Range Storm he ordered earlier and placed a down payment on. The pick-up date for the truck was three weeks away, so he had plenty of time to purchase some more matching outfits. Having used 90% of the money he had in his savings account for the down payment and the clothes, Peaches had made arrangements to go to the boutique tomorrow to pick up the goods for Shadrack and the advance portion of his fee, that way he could replace the money he spent today.

Still hyped from the day's events, Peaches began going through his mental black book trying to see whom he would invite over tonight to scratch his itch. "El! That's who it will be tonight." Peaches decided out loud. El was a thirty-year-old construction worker, who was born and raised in Brooklyn. Peaches and El went to high school together, but had just started having sex about a year ago. Peaches never knew El was in the life until one night when they ran into each other at Juniors Restaurant. Peaches had gone upstairs to use the bathroom and a second later El came in… and the rest is history.

El was also a part of a group called 235. The brothers that made up 235 portrayed to society that they were straight, but in all reality, they were as gay as jay birds. The thing Peaches loved about El was that he wasn't afraid to experiment. El's famous saying is "I'll give it a try or two". Peaches hoped he was ready, because tonight would at least be a three rounder. Nothing could stop Peaches now; or so he thought.

Chapter 22

Four weeks later, at 2:30 am on a Saturday, Precious was riding shotgun in Peaches brand spanking new lime green Rover. They had just left the motel where they had just done every deplorable thing they could think of to Shadrack and Willie… and got it on tape. The night before, Preme had called Peaches as if he was psychic with instructions for after the meeting with the Rev's. Following instructions, Peaches had the truck in route to Harlem where he was to go to the same exact place he had so long ago taken the first video. Being that Preme was incarcerated, he wouldn't be there personally to take the tape, as he had before. Now, his right-hand man Shannon would be there to get the package.

Shannon was a 52-year-old mack that didn't look a day over 40. Shannon had met Preme when he was a foster kid, took a liking to him and took him under his wing. Preme was now a millionaire, thanks to Shannon's guidance. Peaches, like everyone else in the Tri-State area, knew who Shannon was, but never had any dealings with him. Peaches hoped Shannon was an old freak and that he would take a liking to him, that way he wouldn't have to hustle if they hooked up.

Shannon was the type of cat who would take care of his, and that's just what Peaches needed. A dude who had plenty of money; and him being a legend in the community didn't hurt. As Peaches drove, he reached into his Coach duffle bag and retrieved the video that he had just secretly recorded at the motel. "Here, put this in that metal lock box under your seat." Peaches told Precious, as he handed him the video. Precious in turn did just that and handed Peaches the key to the box.

Barry Alston Ray

"I'm sure glad this shit is over." Precious stated, as he got comfortable in the soft leather seats.

"Me too, but hey, thirty thousand ain't bad at all. Fifteen for you, and fifteen for me."

"Shit, for having to deal with those two nasty ass devils, they should have paid us $100,000" Precious stated. Peaches almost lost control of the truck at the mention of a hundred thousand. Was Precious sending an indirect message that he knows about his seventy-five and the twenty-five that he was supposed to get, thought Peaches? Peaches concluded that there was no possible way Precious could know, and there was no way he could find out.

"Chile, a hundred thousand would be lovely right now. But even that ain't enough for putting up with those two. Precious, they should give us an Oscar for our performances tonight; fuck Halle Berry." The two high-fived each other and broke out laughing.

"I know that's right. But you have to admit, Willie wasn't at all bad; he's a handsome man."

"Yeah, but just knowing the foul shit he does, especially to kids, and being a pastor on top of it. In my book, that makes him fucking ugly all over."

"Chile, you ain't neva lied. Just remember, you can't do foul shit to people and it not come back to you; she's called Karma!" Again, Peaches had to shake off the thought that Precious was talking specifically about him. He was glad that he had finally reached the spot, and was now looking for a parking space. The only parking Peaches could find was right in front of the store, which meant he had to walk around the block to get to the back entrance.

"Okay Precious, I should be no more than 15 minutes, 20 tops. I'm leaving everything in here, including my cell. Keep the doors locked. If someone comes by and attempts to play themselves, just get on the phone and call for help. I'll be right back."

"I got you. Just don't take all night."

With that, Peaches opened the door and jumped out the truck with the metal lockbox tucked under his arm. Once the door was closed, Peaches waited to make sure Precious locked the door. Once Precious secured the door, Peaches took off walking rapidly around the block. When Peaches finally made his way to the back entrance, he did a fast-signaled rap on the door and waited. A few seconds later, the door cracked just enough for Peaches to slide into the dark room. Once inside, the door shut and was locked quickly. A light came on and Peaches was staring into the face of the ever so sexy Shannon.

"Why don't you have a seat Peaches. It is Peaches right?" Shannon asked.

"Yes, it is… and thanks. I don't really have a bunch of time, cause I have my sister in the truck."

"I take it you're referring to Precious right?"

"Um, ain't nothing more attractive in a man than intelligence." Peaches flirted.

"Intelligence is all it takes?"

"Well, no, having some hidden treasures and talents is always a plus."

"We'll have to explore that later. But for now, let's get down to business. I see you have the box." Peaches took the box from under his arm, shook it one time, letting

Shannon know that the video cassette was inside. Then placed it on the desk that separated them. "Alright, I'm assuming there's a tape in there. Now, let's take care of the payment. You received twenty-five in advance, so I have an additional fifty for you and twenty-five for Precious."

Shannon produced and handed Peaches two envelopes filled with money. "You can count it if you'd like. The bills are wrapped in bundles of ten thousand. And of course in Precious' envelope, the small stack is five thousand."

"No, counting won't be necessary. I know Preme nor you would cheat anyone; I trust your word."

"Now that business has been completed, why don't you tell me a little about yourself, and whether or not you have someone at home waiting on you after a long night's work." Peaches sat back in the chair, crossed his leg over the other in a suggestive manner and began speaking, laced with nothing but charm.

****

Outside, while Peaches was inside getting his flirt on, Precious was waiting in the Rover silently wishing that Peaches would hurry the hell up. Precious figured he could get home, call Malik over and have time to get refreshed before he gets there. While Precious was sitting there planning, Peaches cell phone, which had been sitting on the dashboard, began to ring. "Hello?" Precious stated after grabbing the phone and pressing the "answer" button.

"Peaches?" Preme asked, wondering if he had dialed the wrong number.

"No, this is Precious. Peaches should be back momentarily."

"Okay Precious, how did things go tonight?"

"And who is this asking?"

"The one who hired your ass, as well as paying you. I take it you're in Harlem, and Peaches has gone to make the drop and collect your fees?"

"Okay Mr. Man. Your take was correct, and things went perfectly tonight, just as planned."

"That's good. Alright, tell Peaches I called and said that I appreciate your hard work." Preme stated, emphasizing hard.

"No problem Mr. Man. Think of me when you have some more work."

"Sure will. You take care, and don't spend that twenty-five g's all in one place." Preme said and hung up the phone before Precious could respond.

"That sneaky, triflin', lyin', cheatin' ass bitch!" Precious declared as he threw the phone back on the dashboard. "So, you wanna cheat me out of ten g's of my hard-earned money? I don't think so; it's on bitch. Precious slid from the passenger seat over to the driver's seat. He sat there, waiting for Peaches to showing his lying ass face.

****

Thirty minutes later Peaches exited the shop from the same door he entered. Before leaving, Peaches had gone to the bathroom and removed ten thousand from Precious' envelope. Now, as he was heading back to the truck, he convinced himself that the ten thousand was rightfully his. After all, Preme was his connect, as well as Shadrack and the Willie Laeitgood character. Peaches picked up his pace, ready to get home and have this night be over.

Finally Peaches turned the corner and headed to the truck. Peaches noticed that Precious was no longer in the passenger seat, but in the driver's seat. "That bitch couldn't wait to drive my truck" Peaches said to the stars and the wind. When Precious saw Peaches coming, he started the truck. Peaches walked over to the passenger side, opened the door and hopped in. "You've been itching to drive the Range, huh bitch? Just be easy with her."

"I haven't been itching. I just figured that you needed a rest, and I know exactly where I parked my ride. So it would just be easier for me to drive." Precious explained.

"Yeah, whatever bitch."

Precious guided the truck down the streets of Harlem, in route back to Queens where his car was parked on a dark deserted block by a bunch of warehouses. Precious had decided to park there, that way if things had gotten funky at the motel, his ride could never be placed at the scene. Yea, he had to walk twenty-five minutes to get to civilization and then caught a cab a block away from the motel. But it was better to be safe than sorry. "So, how did things go with the drop and the pick-up?" Precious asked, hoping Peaches was gonna keep it honest.

"Things went just as planned. It took a lil longer than I expected because Shannon insisted that I count the money; thirty thousand just like we were promised. Here's your half." Peaches said and handed him the envelope containing the fifteen that he had concealed in his jacket. Precious took the envelope and placed it in his jacket pocket. It was still unbelievable to Precious, that this heifer, who was supposed to be his friend, had tried to jack him for a measly ten g's. It wasn't so much the money, but rather the principle of the matter. Precious put his foot down on the gas pedal, because he was anxious to confront this bitch but he wouldn't do it while he was driving. When Precious was five minutes from where his car was parked, he began a subtle dialogue.

"Ya know, I think they should've paid us a bit more than thirty g's. First off, we really had to act like we were enjoying those assholes to get them loose. Then our black asses are on the video just the same as theirs. And there's no telling where those videos will end up. I just think we got cheated. What do you think?" Peaches didn't really know what to think about anything, other than going to bed. Maybe an afternoon booty call with El and trying to get Shannon; Peaches knew there was no possible way Precious could know about the extra ten g's, so he wouldn't even entertain the thought anymore.

"I think I probably could've held out for more, but at the time, I thought it was a good deal." Precious turned onto a deserted street with nothing but warehouses. "What the hell possessed you to park way over here in the damn woods?" Peaches inquired.

"It's called being safe. If shit got hectic, it's easy to find someone from their license plate number. If there's no car, then there's no trace. Which means… you can't find me. You dig what I'm saying?"

"Yeah, I guess you're right about that. I need to think like that next time." By this time, Precious was slowing the truck, then brought it to a complete stop 12 ft. from his two-year-old Beemer.

"Come on, I brought you a gift back from my Cancun trip, and I'm not carrying it for you. So let's go." Precious stated as he opened the driver side door and got out.

"You really are a thoughtful bitch. Let's go, I wanna see what you brought me!" Peaches exclaimed, sounding too much like a damn broad. He jumped out the truck and followed Precious to his ride.

Precious reached the trunk of his car, inserted his key, but did not turn it to open it immediately. "Okay, turn your back, cause it's a surprise. Plus, I wanna see the expression on your face when you turn around and see what I have for you."

"Bitch, you are really too many things." Anxious to see what he had coming, Peaches turned his back with both hands on his hips in an impatient stance. Once Peaches had turned around, Precious opened his trunk. He removed a custom-made steel bat from his trunk. Precious was from the old school; he believed that beating a bitch to death with a bat was better than shooting or stabbing them. Plus, it was almost impossible to trace. All you had to do was thoroughly clean the bat afterwards.

Precious made sure he had a nice tight grip on the bat, and that he was in the proper position. "Okay, you can turn around now." Peaches swung around with excitement in his face. But it changed as the bat was milliseconds away from catching him on the left side of his face. Precious had swung the bat so hard that when impact was made, you could hear bones shattering throughout the quiet and deserted block. "You like jacking people for their money huh bitch?" Precious said as the bat caught Peaches, and he yelled in pain hitting the floor. "Where's the rest of my money you, triflin bitch?" Precious asked as he stood over Peaches with the bat raised, ready to swing.

"What are you talking about?" Peaches asked between sobs, still trying to cover his dirty deed, which only infuriated Precious more. "You still wanna play games huh? Well hold this." Precious said, as he commenced to rain blows with the bat over Peaches body. "A lousy ten g's, when you already made seventy-five thousand, you greedy bitch. No, Precious ain't having it!" When the rain of blows first started, Peaches cried out in pain from each one. Now, each blow was more brutal than the one before. And by the sixth or seventh hit, Peaches was unconscious. "It's a shame your greedy ass had to die over ten thousand." Finally, after what seemed like forever, Precious stopped and looked down at the limp bloody Peaches lying on the ground. There was no doubt in his mind that he was dead.

Precious bent down and carefully removed the envelope Peaches had concealed in his jacket. Precious checked the envelope and was not surprised to see the money. Precious stood, placing the envelope in his pocket along with the other one. He then went to the truck, gave it a quick search finding nothing else of importance. Precious wiped off everything he touched. Once he was finished, he walked back to his car, stopping once to look at Peaches lying in a pool of blood. Precious walked over to him and from deep down within, he spit directly in Peaches face. Precious got in his whip and took off, never looking back, while Peaches laid there unconscious but still breathing. Peaches was that way when a few of the weekend warehouse workers came to work and found him lying there. Precious had talked earlier about being safe, yet he failed to make sure Peaches was really dead. Down the line, that mistake would cost him severely.

****

While Ant was preparing for his upcoming return to society, and while Peaches was lying in a hospital bed, Precious was out and on a mission. Precious was in Harlem, going to all the spots where Shannon was known to be. Now that Peaches was out of the way, he had to make sure Shannon and his partner knew who to contact when work was needed. With all the spots checked, only to find Shannon wasn't at any of them. Finally, Precious pulled up to the last spot on his list. A little candy store on St. Nicholas Ave, right off of 125th street.

There were no patrons inside the store, and only one employee was behind the counter; an old wrinkled black man. He had to be at least 90-years-old. Precious wondered why the hell anyone would leave their establishment in his care, and at his age. Precious knew he probably couldn't see or hear that good. "What can I help you with?" The old man asked Precious, when he approached the counter.

"Yes, I'm looking for Shannon. Is he around?" Precious yelled, taking his time with each word. Hoping the old timer got it the first time, so he wouldn't have to repeat himself.

"What the hell are you yelling for, you high or something?" Precious wished the floor would just open and swallow him, because that's just how foolish he felt.

"I'm sorry, I just thought…"

"Yeah, you thought! He thought he had to piss, but instead he had to shit! So, you say you're looking for Shannon?"

"Yes, sir I am" answered Precious, who was a bit confused by what the old man just said.

"You have an appointment?

"No but…"

"Well how the hell you know he wanna see you?" The old times asked looking Precious up and down, making him feel like a two-year-old.

"It's really important, and I just figured that he would be able to see me for a few moments. If not, I understand and I will try to set up an appointment." Precious stated, hoping the old man would assist him today, and not make him have to come back another day.

"Whatcha say your name is?"

"Precious"

"What kind of God-awful name is that? Your mammie was probably high when she names you. Go figure" the old timer said, as he moved towards two phones on the wall behind the counter. One of the phones was a standard rotary dial phone, while the other looked the same; with the exception that there was no rotary dial, nor any buttons to push. The old timer picked up the phone and waited. "Yeah, there's a he/she out here, says his name is Precious. Said he needs to see you." Precious couldn't believe what he just heard. Here he was underestimating the old guy, and he was just as sharp and brazen as a twenty-year-old. "No, I don't see no Peaches with him. It came alone." Precious would have gone completely off for being referred to as "it". But for some reason, this old man had him in check, and didn't even know it.

"If you say so." He hung up the phone. "Behind that door" he said, while pointing to a door at the back of the tiny store.

"Thank you very much." Precious stated, and headed for the door. Once precious got there, there was a buzz that gave him access to enter. Precious proceeded through the door, and found Shannon sitting at a desk, covered with money and number slips.

"So, Precious, we meet at last." Shannon stated, as he rose from his seat and extended a hand for Precious to shake.

"Yes, finally" replied Precious as he shook Shannon's hand.

"Do have a seat." Shannon offered, pointing to the old, worn sofa on the side of the desk, as he returned to his seat. "So, you're traveling alone today? Where's your partner in crime; Peaches?" Shannon asked, giving Precious his undivided attention.

"That's one of the reason's I'm here. A couple of days after the job was completed, I got a call from Peach's family informing me that he had been murdered." Precious relayed the news with much sadness and sympathy in his voice.

"What? When? Where?" Shannon asked, totally in shock from what he had just been told.

"He was found beaten to death out in Queens, over by the warehouses. That's all the information known." Precious said.

"Was he robbed or what? You mean there are no clues or leads?"

"His family didn't know, and I didn't ask too many questions."

"They were really taking it hard." Precious said, wiping his eyes with his hand.

"That's really sad. Peaches was good people. You don't find honest and true people like him." It was obvious this mofo didn't know that triflin', thieving bitch. "Well, I'm sorry for your loss as well. I know the two of you were close. He always spoke highly of you."

"Thank you, Shannon. That means a lot to me."

"You said that was only one of the reasons you stopped by, so I'm guessing there's more?"

"Yes, I wanted to give you my information in the event that your partner needs more work done. I need to keep busy, so I'd be more than willing to work whenever I'm needed." Precious said, and handed Shannon a piece of paper taken from his pants pocket. Shannon took the paper and studied the numbers on it.

"I'll be sure to pass it on a relay your message. I think that business y'all took care of is over, but you can never tell what Preme has up his sleeve. But once he hears about Peaches, he may put you on the books to snoop around so that the bastards who did that to him can be dealt with. You have no problems with that right?"

"Not at all! As a matter of fact, I feel it's my obligation to do so."

"I figured you'd feel that way. Now Precious, I wish I could sit here and talk, but as you can see, duty calls." Shannon said, sweeping his arms out over the desk filled with money and slips.

"No problem. I need to be getting back to Jersey anyway." Precious rose from the sofa, as did Shannon from his chair.

"Expect to hear from me or Preme in a few days." Shannon stated, as he extended his hand once again for Precious to shake. After shaking Shannon's hand, Precious walked to the door and Shannon pressed a button to let him out. Precious walked back into the store where the old timer was still sitting behind the counter.

"Thanks again for your help sir." Precious said as he headed to the door leading to the street.

"Damn sissy. Burn in hell!" Precious hightailed it out of the store, away from the creepy old man. As he made his way back to where he had parked his ride, he felt elated because Shannon said that he would be getting a call in a few days. "Bring on the money!" Precious yelled, as he strutted up 125th street.

Chapter 23

Ant woke up bright an early Monday morning feeling refreshed, even after only getting three hours of sleep. He and Preme sat up most of the night cracking jokes and having a good ole time. Ant had since given up trying to get anything personal out of Preme; he was locked up tighter than Fort Knox. Right now, Ant couldn't dwell on Preme and that in which he was withholding. He had more pressing matters swarming in his mind, and the most pressing matter was the fact that tomorrow morning would be the last time he would ever wake up in a jail cell. After ten long years, tomorrow… Ant would be a free man.

So many questions ran through his mind. Would he be able to survive on his own after being locked away for so long? Would he be able to fit back into society? Would he be able to find a job? The questions went on and on. Ant felt somewhat relieved that he had such an amazing support team. Harold & Denise were coming to New York the following weekend. They would have come sooner, and even been there when Ant was released, but everyone decided and felt that Ant needed the first week or so alone after being around people non-stop for ten years; being alone for a few days sounded like Heaven.

Then there was Manny, who had been such a blessing. They had agreed to get together in a few days and Manny said he was going to take Ant shopping, which he was looking forward to. And lastly, there was Preme. Even though Preme still had three months left until his release, he had already done so much for Ant. Thanks to Preme, Ant had a one of a kind hand tailored suit to step out in. With all the accessories to match. Ant was on top of the world. However, other thoughts came to mind as well; all dealing with Sylvia and Shadrack. Ant tried hard not to think about them. Harold and Denise reassured him that they were long gone, never to resurface again.

He was overcome with all the various emotions and feelings racing through him that he slipped out of bed, got on his knees and began to thank God for all his blessings. Ant began to thank God for his goodness and mercy. He thanked him for keeping him strong the past ten years. For the wonderful people in his life; Harold, Denise, Preme and Manny. Ant began asking God to order his steps upon his release. The more Ant prayed and cried out to God, the more he felt an assurance that everything was gonna be alright.

Once he got finished praying, he got up, brushed his teeth, and laid back down. Being that today was his last day, he didn't have to work. CO Simmons had told him he could come out of his cell to hang out, say his good-byes and give away the stuff he wasn't taking with him. Ant had all the stuff he planned to give away stacked up against the wall. Preme had encouraged him to give everything away, with the exception of his Bible, photos and the chain. Preme had assured him that he'd be able to get all new stuff once he was released, and that he didn't need anything out in society that was tainted from being in prison. Preme had already managed to get Ant all of his favorite artist on CD like Patti LaBelle, Oleta Adams, Donny Hathaway, Milira and the list goes on. There was 82 CD's down in the property room, along with his suit. Ant couldn't wait.

As Ant laid there anticipating his forthcoming freedom, his cell opened. Ant continued to lay there thinking Simmons had opened his cell to give him access to hang out on the gallery. "Morgan!" Simmons yelled after waiting a few minutes to see if Ant would emerge from his cell. Upon hearing Simmons call his name, Ant got up, stepped out of the cell and proceeded to the front of the gallery. When he reached the front, Simmons opened the gate, giving Ant access to come off the gallery.

"Two things Morgan." Simmons said, after Ant had stepped past the gate and after Simmons secured the gate. "The woman in the mail room called. There was an envelope delivered overnight for you from some lawyer. You'll get the papers and so forth this evening, when the mail is passed out. She said to tell you that there was a key enclosed. They sent you a receipt and you can pick it up when you pick up your other stuff in the morning." Ant couldn't figure out the meaning to this one. Harold and Denise had sent the keys to Mother Green's house last month; which he had the receipt to pick them up in the morning as well.

"Did she mention the lawyers name?" Ant asked, with his usual look of bewilderment.

"No, she didn't, but don't go racking your brain; you'll find out in a few hours. Ant knew Simmons was right. Wasn't no point in stressing. He would indeed find out soon enough. "Listen Morgan, you're out of here tomorrow and I wanted to let you know that I'm gonna be praying for you." Ant's eyes instantly began to water. Simmons knew what Ant had been through and didn't want the conversation to get too emotional, which Ant was known to do. Simmons continued, with all intents of making this conversation short and sweet. "You were by far the best worker I've ever had. Son, you've been through a lot, but you've come through like a trooper. I wish nothing but the best for you. Professionally, I shouldn't say what I'm about to, but it's in my heart to. If you find yourself out there in need of anything, or just someone to talk to, I'm in the book.

Simmons pointed to his name tag that hung on the left side of his shirt, directly above the pocket. Afterwards, Simmons places his hand out for Ant to shake. Fighting not to let tears spill over, Ant shook his hand.

"Thanks Officer Simmons, that means a lot to me." Ant confessed.

"Just don't bring your ass back here, ya hear?"

"Yeah, I hear ya!"

"Alright, go on down there and get yourself together. Tomorrow will be here before you know it." Once Simmons opened the gate, Ant stepped back on the gallery and made his way down to his cell. Once inside, Ant laid down on the bed still amazed that tomorrow a change would finally come.

****

Around 4 pm that same day, Ant was in his now almost empty cell sitting on the bed watching Oprah. Preme was finally up and could be heard moving stuff around as he was getting ready to prepare his and Ant's last jail meal together. He refused to tell Ant what he was making, but Ant wasn't concerned. Preme was a fairly good cook. Today, Oprah was having a talent contest and some of the singers were pretty damn good. Especially this chunky sister name Lashell Griffin. There was no doubt in Ant's mind that the sister had been singing in the church her entire life. Ant was so engrossed in the show that he was unaware of the CO standing at the gate until he spoke. "Morgan."

ChoirBoy

"Yeah" a startled Ant said, as he turned to face the CO at the gate.

"Mail" the CO said, and dropped a large blue and white envelope on the bars and walked away. Ant reached over and grabbed the envelope. Before going through the contents inside, he looked at the name listed on the sender's box. The envelope was sent by a Henry Guslaw, Esq., and it gave a downtown Park Avenue address. Still not knowing who this lawyer was, or what he wanted, Ant tore the envelope open to put an end to the mystery.

Inside the envelope were two sheets of paper. One was a formal typed letter, and the other was a legal document. Ant read the letter and had to reread it three times before it started to sink in. The letter informed Ant that he was now the proud owner of a two bedroom, fully furnished condominium in Jamaica Estates, Queens. Also that the keys and the deed were enclosed. Ant sat there staring back and forth from the letter to the deed. Suddenly, like a ton of bricks the name of the former owner of the condo was on the deed: Cecil Brown.

"Surprise!" Preme sang. Ant looked up and saw Preme on his gate, looking at him through the mirror he held in his hand.

"Have you gone completely mad? You can't afford to just go throwing around condo's whenever you feel like it." By this time, Ant was on his feet standing at the gate, still holding the letter and deed in his hand.

"To answer your questions, no I'm not completely mad. Just partially. Secondly, I can certainly afford to do what I do. And lastly, I don't just go throwing around condo's whenever I feel like it; but I did just give you mines."

"Why" Ant questioned.

"Because, I never use the damn place. I know you have Mother Green's home, but you might not want to live there. It might be too painful, you know… with the memories and all. Plus, with you getting ready to be a big singing sensation and all, the condo will be better. And Jamaica Estates is a great community… but you know that already.

"What the hell are you talking about? I ain't no big singing sensation."

"I didn't say you are. I said you're about to be."

"And how do you figure that?" A clearly confused Ant asked.

"Oh, I forgot to mention a few things to you; allow me to explain everything." Preme said with a cat like grin on his face.

"Please do. And hurry up, will you?"

"Alright. Are you aware that the Rev. here records every service?"

"I'm not sure if I knew that, but so what?"

"I went to the Rev. and asked him to send a copy of that song you sung in service that day to one of my boys. He got the tape, listened to it and loved what he heard. And now, you have a meeting with him Friday at noon."

"Okay, I must be missing something. Who is your boy?"

"You sure you wanna know all that? Preme asked, knowing good and well Ant was about to explode with curiosity.

"You know what, I can't deal with the games right now." Ant said, clearly getting agitated and turned to walk away from the gate.

"Michael Richards." Preme blurted out, knowing he could no longer keep Ant in suspense.

"You mean Michael Richards from CIA Records?" Ant said as he turned back around.

"The one and only." Ant was about to express doubt and bombard Preme with 100 questions. But one thing Ant had learned was, when Preme stated something, you could take it to bank.

"Yo, I ain't even gonna front. This is unbelievable. But knowing you, it's so.

"Friday at 11:15 am a limo will come to the condo to pick you up. Make sure you represent gear wise; I know you know how to hold your own vocally."

"Yeah, yeah, I'll make sure to go to one of your stores and pick out something crazy." Ant got quiet and just began to reflect on all the things Preme had done for him since their first encounter. Despite the fact that Preme had yet to open up and reveal who he was as Ant had done, Ant realized that people didn't come any better than Preme. "Yo, I don't know what to say. Man, you are a major blessing."

"Look, it's way too early for that sentimental shit. Go get yourself together and let me finish cooking; I'll holla when the food is ready. With that, Preme pulled the mirror in and vanished from the gate. Ant sat down on the bed and began counting his blessings, as tears of joy rolled down his cheeks. Despite Preme thinking that it was too early in the afternoon for emotions, Ant knew otherwise.

****

ile Ant was sitting in his cell waiting for Preme to
n cooking dinner, Peaches was secretly being released
m the hospital. Once Peaches was able to
ommunicate, he had made his family promise that they
wouldn't disclose the fact that he was alive. The only
person outside of his immediate family who was told the
truth was his childhood friend Devon, who Peaches
secretly had a crush on all his life. And he was sworn to
secrecy.

Peaches hadn't informed his loved ones as to what
really happened. Due to the fact that Peaches was
attacked at night and left for dead, they were more than
willing to go along with all his requests believing it was for
the best. Peaches gave instructions to give up and clear
out his apartment. He had also given instructions to sell
his baby; the lime green Rover. He had requested that an
apartment in Staten Island be rented and that his
belongings be taken there. Peaches didn't know anyone in
Staten Island, and that's just what he wanted. He would
have plenty of time to get his strength back and plot his
revenge on Precious. Peaches promised himself that
Precious would pay, even if it was the last thing he ever
did.

****

While Ant was sitting in his cell, and Peaches was being
released from the hospital, Precious was driving his brand
spanking new lavender Lincoln Aviator off the lot. Precious
was so proud of his ride, that he equipped it with
everything. From heated seats, to voice activated
everything. To turn on the radio, all he had to do was give
a verbal command. The thing Precious loved the most
was the custom made 22" rims that were trimmed in the
same color lavender as the jeep. With the money he had

taken off of Peaches, Precious felt it was only right that he treat himself … all in the name of Peaches.

Precious didn't feel not one bit of sorrow over Peaches. After all, the bitch was the one who tried to play him. Now, Precious had not only the money that he worked for; the very same money Peaches tried to steal from him. But he had Peaches cut too. And because of that, he was pushing this proper ride. Little did Precious know, the entire situation with Peaches was far from over. While Precious was out painting the town lavender, Peaches was getting stronger and plotting his revenge.

****

Shadrack and Willie made their way through the crowded terminal of the Las Vegas International Airport. Once they made it outside to the parking lot, it was only a few feet to where Shadrack had parked his car. Once the bags were secured in the trunk, they both got in Shadrack's Benz and drove off. "So, how was London my friend?" Shadrack asked Willie, as they exited the confines of the airport.

"It was seven weeks of pure unadulterated bliss. Man, those London youngsters wore me out. Rather, I wore them out… cause you know I Lae's it good!" Willie stated and busted out laughing.

"Yeah, whatever you say. You shouldn't try to be so modest."

"Shadrack, don't tell me you've become a hater; or are you green with envy?"

Shadrack continued to guide the car and quickly changed the subject, not wanting to hear Willie toot his own horn. "You remember Peaches Willie?"

"How could I forget Peaches & Precious?" Willie stated, as he began to reminisce on the adventure that took place In New York.

"Well, Peaches mother was a member of my church in New York, and remained faithful throughout this whole mess. I call from time to time just to check in on her, even though she doesn't know where we reside now. She insists that when she retires, she's coming to live with Sylvia and I."

"That's heartwarming Shadrack, but what's the point to all of this?" Willie interrupted.

"I called her a week or so ago, and she informed me that Peaches had been beaten and murdered."

"NO! How?"

"Apparently he was robbed, beaten, and left for dead in an alley or something."

"Such a waste. What is the world coming to?"

"This nation is going to hell in a handbasket Willie. If God doesn't judge this nation soon, then he has some explaining to do to Sodom and Gomorrah." Shadrack said sternly.

"Preach Preacher; you are so right. Was Precious with him?"

"No, they weren't together at the time."

"Well, do you think you can set up a meeting with Precious once I get my strength back?" We might as well enjoy that before God serves judgement on him as well."

"Amen." Shadrack said in agreement.

ChoirBoy

****

Standing in front of Preme's cell the following morning, this was it. A change had finally come. Last night, after feasting on the typical jail house meal of fried jack mackerel patties, rice with calamari & octopus and biscuits, Preme had insisted that Ant got to bed early. Stating that he would need his rest for society. Ant tried to have a convo, but Preme wasn't trying to hear any of it. Ant had hoped to get some answers out of Preme, all to no avail. Preme insisted that Ant knew enough for now. Ant figured one more attempt wasn't going to hurt. CO Simmons had informed him that his escort would be there to get him soon; Ant had to be escorted to the property room at the front of the jail where all his property was waiting. And where he would change his clothes. After that, he was out the door.

"Don't forget about your meeting on Friday. My man is talking a major million-dollar deal." Preme said.

"I got it man, don't sweat it. Preme, before I break out, please tell me why you refused to open up to me? You don't trust me or something?"

"Ant, I trust you. It's just complicated.

"Morgan be on stand-by. Your escort is on his way." Simmons yelled down the gallery. Ant didn't respond to Simmons. He had a small bag resting at his feet containing his Bible and some photos. He was ready whenever the escort arrived.

"Complicated how?" Ant asked, still seeking answers.

"Complicated in the sense that it's painful."

"I shared a lot of painful stuff with you, but I felt better once I got it out." For a moment, neither one of them said anything. Ant began to think that he had finally got through. "Preme, tell me something. Prove to me that you trust me with something more than just possessions." Again, there was a silence, and it seemed as if Preme's eyes were watery.

"You're not the only who's been hurt by Shadrack."

"Morgan, your ride is here" Simmons yelled.

"What are you talking about Preme?" Ant asked, totally ignoring Simmons.

"My mother got pregnant at a young age while working for Shadrack at his church in Florida."

"Morgan!" Simmons called out again.

"I'm coming!" Ant yelled in response to Simmons, but gave Preme a look that said keep going.

"My mother had already had one son James, and then she popped up pregnant with me. Shadrack must have sensed my mothers' plight. Young with one child and another on the way. Man gone and no money, so he asked my mother to marry him; and she did. Shadrack abused my brother James, just as he did you. James took his life, and my mother left Shadrack before I was born. Even after giving birth to me, she never got over James' suicide; she eventually did the same. I was left to be raised by the streets.

This was too much for Ant to comprehend; thousands of questions began racing through his mind. Like, did Preme know who he was, before he befriended him? Did Preme use him just to get information? There was one question after the next, with no end in sight. Before Ant could begin to try and sort this mess out in his brain, he was interrupted by another yell from Simmons.

"Morgan, your escort said if you're not downstairs in thirty seconds, you're gonna have to spend another night in this place." Ant just stood there in a daze and expressionless.

"Ant, get your bag and go; we'll talk more about this when I get out. Rest assured, that soon after I'm released, Shadrack won't be able to hurt another soul. Bet that." With that, Preme turned away from the gate and Ant. Ant picked up his bag and stood there a second longer. Ant wanted to say something, but didn't know what to say. Ant slowly began walking towards the front of the gallery.

Having made his way off the gallery and to his escort before being left, Ant thought of all the stuff he had just learned. Ant didn't know what was going to happen in the future, but he did know one thing. And that was... this mess was far from over!

About The Author

Barry Alston Ray was born and raised in Corona, Queens. Barry was raised in the Church and began singing as well as directing choirs at an early age. As a teen Barry found himself in the NYS Department of Correctional Services, sentenced to 15 years to life. Barry was released on July 17, 2014, after making his 8th parole board and serving a total of 22 years and 9 months. Today Barry is an accomplished actor, singer/songwriter, published model, business owner and now author. He's just getting started!

ChoirBoy 2:

Vengeance Is Mine

Coming Soon!